IN TRUTH AND LOVE

TRINITY LAKES ROMANCE BOOK TEN

JENNY GLAZEBROOK

CHAPTER ONE

Jodie didn't mind being home alone. Honestly, she didn't. The ability to face loss and loneliness had become her greatest strength.

The problem was, right now she wasn't alone. Four pairs of eyes peered at her from behind the photo frame on her bedroom bookshelf. And they all came from one body. She generally didn't mind spiders, but this one was huge.

One hairy leg lifted. Her breath hitched. If only her friends in the photo could come to her rescue. But they were long gone, just like so many before them.

Any pastor's daughter living her childhood years in a Bible college learned that year after year, friend after friend would leave, taking a piece of her heart with them. But no more. She'd learned to guard her heart, and now it was her turn to leave Trinity Lakes. Her turn to leave the past behind.

The spider twitched. Jodie blinked. She wasn't scared. She was strong and courageous. She was a capable, independent young woman about to become even more independent. Mr. Wolf Spider was just testing her. And thank goodness he'd come out of the woodwork now—literally. She must have disturbed him when she pulled all her old journals from the shelf and packed them into a box to store in the basement—years' worth of journals recording every dream, every prayer, every friendship lost. Only God had remained.

Packing them away was symbolic. She was leaving the past behind. At twenty years of age, she'd finally saved enough to go to NYU and carry out her dream of studying journalism. And, praise God, she'd received a scholarship for the summer intake beginning in May. God had provided for her in every way.

Another hairy leg twitched. She shuddered. How long had Mr. Wolf been hiding in her bedroom?

"Don't you even think about it." She heard the tremor in her voice. Strong and courageous? Who was she kidding? Mr. Wolf was freaking her out.

Lord, please help me here.

What could she do? There was insect spray downstairs, in the laundry room—too far away, even if she made a run for it. The spider would disappear into a moving box the moment she took her eyes off him. Better to face him here rather than alone in a tiny room at NYU.

Besides, being poisoned was a cruel way to go. God cared for the sparrows and that meant He cared for this spider, too.

Mom's car pulled into the driveway. She breathed a sigh of relief and slowly, carefully, one eye still on the spider, pulled her phone from her pocket. She glanced back at the spider between each letter typed to her mom.

In my room. Trapped by spider. Please—

The spider twitched again. She tensed. In a flash of movement, it sprinted along the shelf toward her. Unable to help herself, she screamed. A long, awful sound, loud enough to shake the windows. Who knew she was capable of such a noise? She probably scared herself as much as Mr. Wolf.

Feet pounded on the stairs, too fast to be Mom.

"Josh?" She held a hand to her heart, trying to catch her

breath, desperately scanning for any sign of the spider. Where was it?

Strong arms grabbed her and spun her around. She pushed back on her brother's solid chest, her gaze still focused on the spider, and pointed a shaking finger toward the shelf. "He's in there somewhere. Quick. He'll get away."

"Jodie. Look at me."

The voice was not her brother's. She looked up into concerned, distinctive green eyes.

"Brandon." Her brother's best friend. All the air drained from her lungs. Panic was replaced by a sheepish reality.

"What happened?" Brandon demanded.

An embarrassed giggle escaped.

Confusion washed over Brandon's features. He had grease on his forehead and his dark hair was poking up in all directions. Needed a good cut, really. But his eyes … she'd never seen them this close before. Had avoided ever being this close.

The spider.

She shook herself from his strong grasp. "I was packing. And there's a wolf spider. Huge. Big eyes. Hairy legs. Over there. On the shelf."

Brandon's eyes crinkled in the corners and his lips twitched. Jodie crossed her arms and stepped back, eyes darting from Brandon to the last place she'd seen Mr. Wolf.

"What are you doing here?" She didn't mean to sound accusing, but Brandon witnessing her fear was plain humiliating.

His half smile grew. "I brought your mom's car back after its service, like she asked. She said you could give me a ride back to work."

Oh. She'd forgotten. "How'd you get inside?"

"There's a house key with the car keys. And when I heard you scream …" He moved toward the shelf. "So, this spider …?"

"Mr. Wolf."

He gave her the side-eye. "Mr. Wolf. Right. Would you like me to get rid of him? Or are you friends now?"

"Depends. How would you get rid of him?"

"Take him outside and let him go."

Well, look who'd turned out to be her knight in shining armor. Jodie bit back a smile. No mention of whacking or spraying or slow, cruel deaths. She dipped her head. "I'd be very grateful."

Brandon glanced around the room, then picked up a small box containing letters. "Can I use this?"

"Sure."

So long as he didn't ask about the letters. All from friends who'd moved on, including Hamish. It would be mortifying if Brandon read a letter from the boy she'd had a crush on as a teenager. His parents were on staff at college, so he'd stayed a full five years. Long enough for her to grow attached. He was five years older, but in his first letter to her he'd admitted he wanted to marry a girl like her one day. A Christian girl with a strong Christian heritage. She'd dared to hope he meant her.

But then he'd stopped returning her letters and emails. Out of sight, out of mind. It seemed that was how the world worked. Still, somewhere deep down, she'd dared to hope. She'd turned down any guy interested in her because one day Hamish might remember her.

Except he clearly hadn't, because word around the Bible college was that Hamish was getting married. And Jodie was fine with that. Really. She'd already received news of her scholarship to NYU. And she wasn't the needy child she'd once been. She'd learned to avoid unnecessary connections or ties to anybody other than her own family.

Brandon carefully tipped the letters onto her desk then moved toward her pile of journals on the shelf. Jodie tensed.

"Aha." He slapped the box down and Jodie let out a small

squeak. Brandon smirked at her, then carefully slid the box along the shelf, using one of her journals to seal it.

She shuddered. "You got him?"

"I did, and he's a beauty." He put on an Australian accent. "Long twitchy fangs, beautiful dark eyes … just gorgeous."

Jodie chuckled at his Steve Irwin impersonation. "Did you and Josh practice that accent together?"

Brandon laughed. "Josh doesn't need practice. He inherited it from your mom. And you should've too. Come on, give me a demo."

"No thanks." The last thing she wanted was to give Brandon another reason to laugh at her.

He held up the box. "How about I take him outside, and you can give me a ride back to work?"

"Sure. And thank you."

"No problem." He smiled a pure, genuine smile, and her heart did a funny leap in her chest. Why was he looking at her like that? Like she amused him, but also like … almost like he had feelings toward her. He was Brandon Taylor, king of sarcasm, master of smug looks. Although he'd changed since his mother was diagnosed with cancer and had admitted his father was alive and that she'd been lying all those years. Brandon was kinder now. Less judgmental. Softer, somehow.

Jodie frowned as she slipped on her shoes while Brandon bounded down the stairs two at a time, spider box in hand. Why did he have to do this? Go and be all … well, like this? She was ready to start fresh and leave everything behind. She couldn't afford to feel any connection with Brandon. There were new people to meet. A bright, new future ahead of her. She was leaving the past behind and she was not going to let her brother's best friend slip behind the guard around her heart.

Lord, above all things, help me guard my heart.

Proverbs 4:23. Her go-to verse.

She slid her phone into her pocket and grabbed her car keys

from the hall stand. In the driveway, Brandon stood beside Mom's car, holding out the empty box and her journal. "I put him in the garden across the road."

"Thanks." She grabbed the box and journal.

"Don't worry. I didn't read it."

Thank goodness for that. He unlocked Mom's car but Jodie shook her head.

"We'll take my car. I'll drive."

She saw the hurt flash over his features before he masked it by rolling his eyes. "I'm not going to be reckless Jodie."

"Speeding is reckless." Brandon was a skillful driver, but too confident for his own good. Sure, he might have great reflexes and be a champion video game racer, playing against Josh and his friends in their basement, but that didn't mean it was right to drive that way on the road. Road rules were there for a reason.

"This again?" His face darkened. No more soft, tender looks.

She slid into the driver's seat of her car and held out her hand for Mom's car keys. "Just get in, Brandon."

"This is ridiculous." He let out a huff of frustration as he jerked open the passenger door, tossed the keys into the console, and slid in.

She focused on the road, turning the corners carefully. No doubt he was judging her driving. She might not have his skill, but at least she was sticking to the speed limit.

Should she ask Brandon how he was doing, how his mom was doing? She prayed for his mother often, but she couldn't tell him. That would be creating connection and opening herself up to loss again.

She was aware of his every movement, aware of his larger-than-life presence in the car, the smell of fuel and oil on his clothes.

He broke the silence. "What will you do if a spider turns up in your room when you're in New York?"

Was he having a go at her independence? Implying she couldn't survive without her family? She might be the youngest and the least of the Ladan family, but she would manage just fine.

"I have God." She pulled up in front of Trinity Lakes Auto Repairs and looked over at him. "Sorry. That came out a bit defensive."

"You think God would carry a spider downstairs for you?" His mouth tugged up at the corners. "Although I've no doubt all heaven heard your scream."

Jodie bit her lip but her smile escaped anyway. "Maybe He'll send a real angel to rescue me next time."

"I was rescuing the spider, not you. He's probably deaf now, poor thing."

She laughed. "Just when I start to think you might actually be nice …"

He grinned. "I am nice." He opened his door and met her gaze, his green eyes capturing hers. "And Jodie, I know that whatever you do, wherever you go, you'll do well. You always do."

He closed the door and sauntered into the workshop.

Jodie watched until he was out of sight. What was she supposed to make of him? She wanted to believe he meant what he said, but she didn't fully trust him. She'd heard him make fun of people one too many times. Not recently, since he'd found out the object of his most violent ridicule, the local trash collector known as the Junk Man, was actually his father, but still …

Lord? She sighed and put her car into gear. It didn't matter. Her future was in New York, far away from Trinity Lakes and Brandon Taylor and his dark good looks and captivating green eyes.

CHAPTER TWO

Brandon refused to look behind him as he walked back into the auto workshop. He needed to compartmentalize. Put Jodie Ladan from his mind. He sighed. Easier said than done. Seeing her today, all cute and on edge, had done something to his heart. This was the first time he'd seen Jodie anything but composed. Imagine her screaming at a spider. It seemed she did have a vulnerable side after all. He liked that she'd allowed him to help her. It gave him hope that maybe she didn't see him as beneath her, as having nothing to offer. But she was leaving, so it didn't matter what he felt.

"Brandon?" His boss came into the workshop. "Would you mind looking at this car that's come in? Susannah says there's some kind of rattle."

"Susannah?" Brandon lifted a brow. "Gilbertson?"

"Yep." Bruce nodded toward the car in the next bay over. Brandon grinned. A brand-new Lexus shone at him, winking in the light streaming through the window. The hood was already up, and Brandon was drawn over like a magnet to metal. He whistled. The engine was a work of art. Beautiful. Powerful. He ran a hand along the edge of the hood, admiring the paint job.

What would the snobby rich woman think if she knew Bruce had left her vehicle in his hands?

"Couldn't see anything wrong with the engine," Bruce said. "You might need to take it for a drive."

Brandon grinned. "Of course."

"Just don't get a speeding ticket or anything that will come back on me."

Brandon frowned. Why did everyone think he lacked judgment? He knew when and where it was safe to push the boundaries. Driving was his passion, cars his expertise. He could handle a car better than anyone else he knew. What was the issue? Even the supervisors at Spokane County Raceway were impressed by his driving whenever he went for a few laps on their circuit. They didn't criticize his driving. Why couldn't everyone else value one of the few things he was actually good at?

Jodie was his greatest critic. Too fast, too reckless, overconfident, foolhardy, hubristic. Yes, she'd used that word. She was a walking dictionary, and never had a good word to say about his driving. If he was honest, it stung. He had great reflexes. He had perfected skills most drivers could only dream of. He had his grandfather to thank for that. His only good memory of the gruff old man was being taken to the local racetrack for his seventh birthday. He remembered Grandpa's uncharacteristic grin, the sparkle in his eyes, and the way they had connected as the professional race car driver had spun them around a corner. They'd caught their breath in unison.

"This is how a real man drives," Grandpa had said, eyes sparkling beneath his bushy brows.

The driver chuckled, looking over his shoulder at Brandon. "You want to be a race car driver when you grow up?"

"Yes," Brandon had said, and Grandpa looked proud.

Being an auto mechanic wasn't quite the same, but Brandon didn't have the money to carry out his childhood dream.

Besides, he didn't need a racetrack to drive with skill. And there was something satisfying about repairing cars for customers, keeping them in good working order.

He slid into the front seat of Susannah's Lexus and closed his eyes. What would Susannah say if she knew he'd sat in her car, taken it for a drive? Susannah despised him, the son of her ex-husband's disdained cousin, the woman she'd disowned before he was even born. He was still guilty by association. Never good enough.

Mom. His smile faded as he turned the car across the stone bridge that led out of town. Mom wasn't doing well. He hated watching cancer drain the life from her body. He'd begged God for a miracle time and time again.

As he came off the bridge, he picked up speed. There was the sound, a slight rattle. Susannah hadn't been imagining it. He slowed, and the rattle did too. He knew that sound. With one hand on the wheel, eyes still on the road, he reached up and felt above the rearview mirror. There. A special compartment. He fiddled with the latch and opened it, feeling inside. He lifted out a pair of sunglasses and the rattle stopped. He chuckled and set the glasses in the console before turning around and heading back to the workshop.

The car glided around corners then purred back into the work bay. He glanced at the pair of Ray-Ban sunglasses, then got out.

He opened the hood for one final check. He'd done his best the way he always did. He'd known from childhood that little was expected from him, so he had a lot to prove.

"How'd you do?" Bruce called through the door.

"Great. Nothing wrong with it." Brandon lowered the hood, confident everything was as it should be. "The rattling sound was her sunglasses."

Bruce chuckled as he sauntered over. "Well, that was an easy fix. You came back quick." He winked. "I honestly thought you might take it for a really good run."

Maybe he should have. He could've taken Dad for a drive. Maybe even invited one of the wild geese Dad rehabilitated. They could have released it down by the lake. Brandon chuckled at the thought of his dad and a goose in Susannah's pristine Lexus.

Jodie's face came to mind again. Her very pretty face, surrounded by golden-blonde hair and lively blue eyes. Eyes that would look at him with disappointment and disapproval if she heard he'd done such a thing. She'd no doubt come up with some appropriate Bible verse to show him up. Something about having Jodie upset with him hurt his heart. It was stupid, the effect she had on him. Always speaking in that way that said she was more spiritual than he was. She'd only been fifteen when he'd first met her, the same day he'd walked into Trinity Life Church and met Josh. As a nineteen-year-old on the cusp of leaving his teens, he'd dismissed the petite Jodie as a child. Big mistake. If only he could write off her gentle reprimands as over-the-top, but he couldn't. That was the truth of it. Even now, five years later, she was like his conscience. A role only God should have in his life.

With a sigh, he closed the hood of Susannah's car. He wouldn't stir the woman, even though it was tempting.

"Look out. Here she comes," Bruce hissed as a woman in high heels and perfectly coifed hair clip-clopped into the workshop's office.

Brandon ducked out of sight as Bruce went to meet her. Let Susannah stay in her pious rich-bubble world and never look his way. It suited him just fine.

What would've happened if his mother had tried to please her rich relatives? Would they have accepted her? Accepted him? Would he have been able to become a professional racer? Afford a Ford Mustang the value of Susannah's Lexus?

Returning to Trinity Lakes when the auto apprenticeship had come up had been a bold move for him and Mom. But they were in it together, just like they were in everything together.

Susannah's voice drifted through the workshop window. He kept his head down, knowing that tone wasn't good. She wasn't happy.

"Where is he?" her clipped voice demanded. "I know he's here."

The sound of heels on the concrete had him tensing.

"Hey, you can't go in there. It's restricted."

The woman ignored Bruce. Brandon set his jaw. How dare she? He wasn't scared of her. Wasn't going to hide.

He stepped into sight and deliberately leaned against the top of her car's door frame. He met her cold gaze.

"*Cousin* Susannah. It's not safe for you to come here. You need to earn the privilege."

She sputtered, looking like she wanted to spit. "I'm not your cousin. We are not connected in any way, shape, or form."

"You married my mom's cousin."

Her face grew red. "And divorced him, as you well know."

Yeah, because she was impossible to live with. He kept that thought to himself. "As Bruce said, this area is restricted, but I can bring your car around for you."

Her eyes rounded as she eyed the grease on his shirt. "You'll do no such thing. Get your filthy hands off my car."

He didn't bother to reassure her that he'd washed his hands and put a clean towel on her pristine seats before driving it.

Bruce stepped in front of her. "I'll bring your car out for you, Mrs. Gilbertson. I'm sorry, but you need to leave this area."

"I can help you out if you like." Brandon moved to her side and held out his arm, the one covered in grease. "Come along."

Her mouth opened and closed and then she swiped at his arm. "Get your filthy, dirty—"

He grinned. "Now, now. That's not a nice way to speak to the man who fixed your car, is it?"

He kept walking out the roller door of the workshop and she followed, stumbling on her heels as she tried to keep up. He stopped and she shook a finger in his face.

"Tell me it isn't true."

He smiled sweetly. "What?"

"Is the Junk Man your father?"

He hadn't expected that. He'd thought she was still talking about him driving her car.

He raised his brows in an innocent expression. "You mean that strange man who cleans up trash down by the lake? Who lives with those filthy geese? How could you say such a thing?"

She eyed him suspiciously.

"Look, Mrs. Gilbertson, everyone knows he's a strange man. A loner. The only girlfriend he ever had sold him out at the request of ..." He looked up as though he was trying to remember. "Oh, that's right. Your ex-husband. I wonder if you know anything about that?"

She blinked, then deflated before his eyes. "It's true?"

He blinked back, eyebrows raised, pretending to take her question as a statement. "You're confessing to me? Telling me you were in on everything that went down that summer twenty-five years ago when the then-mayor, your *husband*—"

"He's not my husband."

"Your husband at the time—asked the environmental officer —whom you accuse of being my father— to doctor records so property developers couldn't outbid him on the land by the lake?"

She went pale. "I'm confessing no such thing."

"Yet you were so worried about the truth coming out that you came to check out what I know. Truth has a funny way of coming out, Mrs. Ex-Gilbertson. And to tell you the truth, I've only just found out the qualified environmental officer who didn't bow to the wishes of an unethical mayor and was demoted to Junk Man, is indeed my father. And I couldn't be more proud of him."

Susannah lifted a shaking hand and he saw her intention. He moved his cheek out of the way of her ringed fingers just in time. She spun on her heel and stalked away.

"Whew." Bruce came out to stand beside him. "Think she'll be back for her car?"

Brandon chuckled. "If not, can I have it?"

Bruce grinned. "If only it worked that way."

CHAPTER THREE

The door to the Bible college office swooshed open. Jodie lifted her lips in a bright smile.

"Good morning. Welcome to Trinity La—" Her smiled dimmed. "Rachel. Hello. How can I help you?"

Rachel Kearn looked around as though expecting to see someone else. She pursed her lips. "Jodie. I thought you were going to New York."

"I am."

The Bible college director's deep chuckle sounded from behind. "That was a very Jesus-like answer."

"Yes, I suppose it was." Jodie turned to grin at Peter, who'd come out of his office.

He smiled at Rachel. "Jodie's working here for another few weeks before she leaves. Come this way."

Rachel followed Peter into his office. What was she doing here? Surely she wasn't planning on studying theology. Or was she being interviewed for the admin position?

She bit her lip. How awkward for Josh if Rachel worked here. Having an ex-girlfriend in his face every day would be awful. Her breath caught. Was that Rachel's plan? To remind

Josh she existed? To come between Josh and his girlfriend, Hallie? She wouldn't put it past Rachel. The woman had never recovered from her infatuation with Josh, which was one of the reasons Jodie kept her at arm's length. She didn't want to be used to get to her brother.

Jodie kept her eye on the closed office door. *Lord, give Peter wisdom.*

The front door swished open again. "Jodes!" Her brother bounced over, grinning. "Fancy seeing you here."

Jodie let out a snort. "Yeah, surprise, surprise." She glanced at Peter's office door. Best to move Josh on as quickly as possible with Rachel in there. "What can I do for you?"

Josh handed over a folder. "All my paperwork for special accommodations. Peter needs to process them."

A look of understanding passed between them. Josh didn't like people knowing he couldn't read, that a traumatic brain injury had left him with a condition called Alexia. It was a miracle he was here, studying theology. He needed special accommodations to help him study, but he'd always wanted to follow in Dad's footsteps. They both had a pastor's heart.

"I hear Rachel's going for your job," he said.

Ha. So nothing was a secret in Trinity Lakes. "I think she's having her interview right now."

Josh winced. "You sure you don't want to stay?"

Jodie looked around the magnificent building that housed the main offices, lecture rooms, and was home to some of the staff. Out the window she caught a glimpse of Lake Wainscott, the sun glistening off the water. It was beautiful. In fact, the whole town of Trinity Lakes was beautiful, but she was tired of staying in the same place, watching helplessly as everyone else came and went from her life. This time it was her turn to say goodbye. Her choice.

"I'm sure."

He grinned. "You don't want to find some pastor to marry? It's a noble profession, you know, being a pastor's wife."

Jodie snorted. "Just because you've found 'twoo wuv' right here in Trinity Lakes doesn't mean I will."

Peter's office door opened as she spoke and Jodie's face warmed. What if he'd heard her poor impression of *The Princess Bride?*

The grin on Peter's face said he had.

"Good morning, Josh." He turned to Jodie. "Rachel's going to spend the day with you today to get a feel for the job and see if it would suit her. Do you mind showing her the basics?"

Jodie shot a look at Josh. He raised an eyebrow and slipped out the door just as Rachel appeared. That was close.

"Um, sure." Jodie passed Josh's folder to Peter, safely away from Rachel's prying eyes. "Josh asked me to give you this."

Thankfully Peter took it straight into his office, and Jodie was left looking at Rachel.

"You're leaving because you haven't found true love?" she asked, eyes wide.

Jodie wanted to groan. "Of course not. Josh was joking." She pulled over a spare chair. "Have a seat, and I'll start by showing you the class schedules."

She felt Rachel's eyes on her as she sat down. "So why are you leaving?"

Jodie opened the file containing schedules. Here's where she needed to give the practical reason, not the emotional one. "Because becoming a journalist has been my dream since I was ten years old." When she'd won a prize at school for her article about the importance of telling the truth. It had even been printed in the Trinity Lakes Gazette, the town's local newspaper. She'd taken the idea from one of Dad's sermons, but still …

Rachel had come a close second in that competition. And had never been as friendly since.

Rachel gave her an assessing look. "Sometimes God redirects our dreams because He has better ones. We need to make sure we're open to that."

Jodie held back a frown. She was a PK. Every pastor's kid knew God's plans were better and that He sometimes re-directed. It's what they'd thought had happened when Josh was tackled so hard he ended up with a brain injury. But God had still allowed Josh his dreams. His calling had never changed.

She forced herself to smile at Rachel. "Not if He's the One who gave us the dream in the first place."

"But how can you know it was Him? How can you know you're not being deceived by your own selfish ambition?"

Wow. Jodie tried to speak, but nothing came out.

Rachel gave her a knowing look. "I always thought you'd end up with Hamish. What happened with him?"

"We were friends. He and his family left for the mission field. He's getting married soon." Not that it was any of Rachel's business.

"I know, but it was so obvious you had a crush on him. I really thought you'd keep in touch and end up together."

Jodie gritted her teeth. "We were just teenagers." What was it with Trinity Lakes? Could nobody have any secrets?

Rachel tapped her chin. "Then I wondered about you and Brandon. With this whole love-hate thing you've got going on, I thought maybe you're just trying to hide your real feelings from each other."

Jodie tried to breathe. "No … no, that's not it at all." She couldn't fall for Brandon Taylor. Wouldn't. He might be twenty-four years old, but he was still immature in the faith. And she was going to New York. Her place was far away from here.

"Just don't let pride keep you from 'true love.'" Rachel imitated Jodie's earlier impression of *The Princess Bride.* "I certainly wouldn't be."

Uh-oh. Rachel wouldn't try to win Josh back, would she? Hallie was perfect for Josh. Hallie was Jodie's one childhood friend who'd returned to Trinity Lakes. At first, she'd thought God had brought Hallie back to be the friend she'd prayed for, but it soon became clear He'd brought Hallie back for Josh. She was happy for her brother, happy for all her family, even if her sister, her own sister, didn't respond to her calls anymore. Esther was too busy with her teaching position in Spokane and her boyfriend Mark, the school principal. But that was okay. Soon Jodie would be busy too, with her own new life in New York.

CHAPTER FOUR

Brandon walked into church to see Josh sitting in his usual place up the back, Hallie by his side. He missed the way he and Josh used to sit there together and watch people come in. They'd store up intel on their quirks, the things they said, to discuss later. Perhaps they'd acted like silly kids, but it had made him feel like he had a brother.

Hallie turned to see him and gave a bright smile—if only he could find reason to dislike her—and Josh slapped him on the back.

"Brando. How are you? How's your mom?"

He shrugged. No miracle to report. It was discouraging having to repeat that she was "not so good" to every person. He was grateful for the full-time nurse caring for her now. The woman was a godsend.

"She's not any better?" Hallie asked, and the compassion in her eyes made his heart hurt.

"Not yet." He slid into the row beside Josh.

Hallie's brilliant blue eyes misted and Josh squeezed her hand. Brandon looked away. He was glad for Josh, truly glad, but he missed the closeness they'd shared before Hallie came along. The Ladan family still tried to include him, invited him for meals, made him feel welcome, but it felt awkward going to their house now Josh had moved out and Hallie had moved in. So much in his life had changed in such a short time.

He focused on the church entry.

Jodie walked in, her blonde ponytail bouncing, followed closely by Rachel Kearn who was struggling to keep up with her.

"If God has someone for you, nothing and no one can get in the way of that." Rachel was talking fast.

Jodie was smiling, but Brandon saw the tightness in her jaw. Then, without warning, she dropped into the tiny space beside him at the end of the pew, almost landing in his lap.

Whoa. Her leg squished against his and he slid along to make space. Jodie wasn't the affectionate type. She'd always carefully kept her distance.

Rachel glanced at them, then her gaze settled on Josh and Hallie before she moved quickly to the front of the church.

"What was that about?" Brandon asked.

Jodie gave the slightest shake of her head but didn't answer.

"Why are you sitting here?" He nudged her. "I thought you said only troublemakers sat in the back row."

She winced. "I did, didn't I? Well, ironically, today I'm here to avoid trouble."

"I'm not trouble?"

"Always. But you're a known quantity of trouble."

His heart jumped at that smile. He scowled to hide it. "So what kind of trouble are you avoiding?"

She leaned close. "I'll tell you later."

He tried not to let her closeness affect him. Tried not to feel sad that Jodie Ladan leaving was yet another change he needed to adjust to.

Brandon tried to concentrate on Theo Ladan's message but couldn't focus. Not with the pastor's daughter sitting so close beside him. He leaned forward in the pew and rested his hands on his knees. Hands stained with grease and oil. He'd scrubbed his hands, but he couldn't get rid of it all. Maybe Leah had something in her organics shop that would work. Something that wouldn't leave them so dry and cracked.

He slid a glance sideways at Jodie. She had a small smile on her face, clearly captivated by the sermon. Oh, to be so good. To have such a strong Christian heritage and find it so easy to live for God.

For Brandon, every day was a challenge. Striving to learn how a good Christian lived. Working to break harmful generational patterns, struggling to deserve the love the Ladan family so freely showered on him.

He'd failed spectacularly, of course. He'd ridiculed the Junk Man for years, having no idea the man was his father. Luke McAffrey. He gritted his teeth. Every time he thought he'd forgiven his mother for her lies, the bitterness, the disappointment came back, just like the stains on his hands. Seventy times seven he was meant to forgive. He loved his mother, but he still felt betrayed. Was it okay if the seventy times seven to forgive his mother was used for the one thing over and over? Or did he need to reserve some of that forgiveness for himself? God knew he needed it.

Before he knew it the service was over and they were standing for their last song. Minutes later two couples stood before him. Local rancher Jackson Reilly and his fiancée Lexi. Josh Ladan and his girlfriend Hallie. And there was Jasper who ran the local hardware store standing beside Ellie Reilly, the young woman who was managing the reopening of the local historical museum. Surely not them too? Everyone seemed to be coupling up. All good Christian people. It would be nice to dream of marrying a lovely Christian girl one day, but he couldn't expect that. He might be a Christian but he didn't really fit here. There were so many people with a strong Christian heritage. People who knew all the rules and expectations and hadn't sinned any more than telling a lie or stealing a cookie once or twice. People who knew their Bible by heart and were genuinely nice.

"You coming to Joe's Diner?" Jackson asked.

See. Nice enough to include a misfit like him. "Sure."

Ellie looked at Jodie. "You want to come too?"

Jodie always said no. He'd never understood the way she kept to herself. But to his surprise, today she said yes. Maybe she wanted to say goodbye to everyone before she left for New York.

Josh turned to Brandon. "Can you give her a ride? Hallie and I need to drop in and grab something she left at home."

Brandon was flung back to the present. "Um… I don't think that's a good idea."

"Why not?"

"Jodie doesn't like my driving."

"So she says, but —"

"Guys!" Jodie waved a hand in front of their faces. "I'm right here."

Brandon bit his lip. The last thing he wanted to deal with today was conflict and having Jodie in his car would inevitably lead to that.

"I can take her," someone said. They all turned to see Rachel. Jodie shook her head. "No, it's fine. I'll go with Brandon."

Rachel's eyebrows lifted, and a knowing look filled her face. She mouthed something, and Josh barked out a laugh.

"Let's go," Jodie said.

Before Brandon knew what was happening, she'd grabbed his hand and pulled him away, down the church steps, across the church parking lot, and toward his truck. He drew in a deep breath. What on earth had Rachel said to incite a reaction like this?

The moment they reached his truck, Jodie dropped his hand. "Sorry about that." She avoided his gaze.

He searched her face. "What did she say?" He opened and closed his fingers. There'd been nothing romantic about Jodie grabbing his hand, but he had to admit it warmed him to his core. He'd always been careful around her, keeping his distance, avoiding contact, respecting her, but she'd initiated the connection. He knew it was because driving with him was the lesser of two evils, but at least he was no longer the greatest evil. He'd take the promotion.

She sighed. "If you must know, she said 'true love.'"

Oh? "She thinks you're in love with me?"

"No. Oh, I don't know."

He grinned. "Don't worry. Everyone knows you hate me." That she was too good for him. Too spiritual.

Her mouth opened in a look of horror. "That's not true."

"Well, they definitely know you're only coming with me today because I'm the lesser of two evils." He opened his truck and climbed in.

She didn't argue, but he didn't expect her to. Jodie was always honest. Sometimes brutally honest. She was going to be a brilliant journalist.

CHAPTER FIVE

Jodie looked across at Brandon as she fastened her seat belt. If only she could tell him the big news—that Josh and Hallie had become engaged yesterday afternoon. They said they wanted to announce it to their friends at lunch today, but Brandon had been Josh's best friend for years. Didn't he deserve to know at the same time as family? They'd tried to call Esther, but she hadn't answered her phone. They'd called her boyfriend Mark too, and he'd said he'd get Esther to call back. But she hadn't.

She fiddled with the bracelet on her wrist — the one Esther had made for her before she moved to Spokane. They should wait. Esther and Brandon deserved to know before everyone else.

"Jodie?" Oh. Brandon had the engine running and was looking at her, concern furrowing his brow.

"Did you say something?"

"It doesn't matter." He shook his head. "Are you really that stressed about my driving? You can drive if it makes you feel better."

He'd let her drive his truck? "No, it's fine. I was thinking about something else."

"You sure?" He put his truck into gear.

"I'm fine as long as you don't drive like a maniac."

He frowned as he pulled out of the parking lot and onto the street. "I never drive like a maniac. I drive like a professional who doesn't need a racetrack to display his skill."

"Yeah, but there are road rules. And Romans tells us to follow the laws of the land." She bit her lip. Brandon had once accused her of preaching at him, the day he found out the truth about his father. It had shocked her to realize he was right. She toned it down. "I know you can handle your speed,"—well, apart from that time he'd slid on the ice last Thanksgiving— "but other people can't."

He chuckled. "Then perhaps other people shouldn't be on the road."

Jodie pursed her lips. Why couldn't Brandon see that driving a car was like holding a loaded gun? Lives were at stake. His blasé attitude was dangerous. His driving was a constant source of contention between them, and she didn't want to add to his burdens.

"Get me safely to Joe's Diner and I'll be happy."

He nodded, his capable arms resting on the steering wheel. She looked away. "I still want to know about this trouble you were avoiding," he said.

Her gaze shot back to him. "What trouble?"

"In church. With Rachel."

She sighed. "I think Rachel still has feelings for Josh. And she's going for my job at the Bible college. Where she'll be with Josh every single day."

"Well there's one way to fix that." Brandon grinned. "Stay."

Jodie laughed. "No, it's time for me to go. I'm an adult, and I've depended on my family long enough. It's time to fly the nest, follow my dreams, follow God's plan for my life. Maybe one day I'll be a foreign correspondent in some war-torn country, able to bring light and truth to the world."

"Big dreams." He glanced at her, then back to the road.

Hurt filled her chest. "You think they're unachievable?"

He pulled up on the street outside the diner and looked over at her. "Definitely not. If anyone can do it, you can. But I hope you never forget the value of what you have."

"Meaning?"

"The support of a loving family."

Oh. What could she say to that? Brandon had gone his whole life without the support of a loving family. True, he'd had his mother, but she had manipulated him for her own purposes. And he hadn't even known his father until recently.

But her family wasn't as close and supportive as he'd like to believe. Esther had left and forgotten about them altogether once she got herself a job and a boyfriend—something Jodie wouldn't do when she left. She'd call at least once a week and make sure her family were still involved in her life.

Other couples were already entering Joe's Diner. Jodie glanced at Brandon, walking strong and tall beside her, hands in his pockets. What would he do if she reached over and slipped her arm through his?

She swallowed and pushed the ridiculous thought aside. Leaving must be affecting her more than she'd realized. Or maybe it was Josh and Hallie's engagement. Hallie had been one of the special childhood friends she'd lost. But God had brought her back to Trinity Lakes. Brought her back to her, to Josh.

Josh waved at them as they came in the door. "Hey, Brando, Jodes, what took you so long? I saved you seats."

Great. She'd be sitting beside them when the engagement was announced. Right in the line of fire.

Jackson fell into the seat across from them, Lexi right by his side. "I've been desperate for a decent burger all week."

Lexi patted the cowboy's hand. "Why didn't you tell me? I would've made you one."

"I know, I know, but you work hard enough as it is." He smiled into Lexi's eyes with such tenderness that Jodie's throat burned. What was wrong with her today? Everything was making her emotional.

When the table was full and everyone had ordered, Josh cleared his throat. "Hey, guys, I have an announcement to make."

Jodie tensed and her neck began to ache.

Everyone followed Josh's gaze to where Hallie was pulling something from her purse. Jodie knew what it was.

Josh beamed at his fiancée. "I have asked Hallie to be my wife. She said yes."

Hallie slid on the beautiful engagement ring.

A gasp went up. Followed by exclamations, cheers, congratulations, and hugs. Jodie watched Brandon. He didn't look surprised. He even managed a smile. But something in his eyes was sad.

She nudged him with her elbow. "You okay?"

He cleared his throat. "Of course. A blind man could see that coming."

"A blind man might hear a speeding car coming at him, but it doesn't hurt any less when it hits."

His expression darkened. She'd used the wrong analogy.

"Sorry. I wasn't having a go at your driving."

He nodded once and looked away.

She bit her lip. Once he would have come back with a biting comment, but he was different these days. He looked troubled and lost. Not that she blamed him. His mother was sick. Very sick. And she understood the betrayal he felt when his mother had hidden the truth about his father from him. He had a lot to work through.

Jackson told a joke and the rest of the table laughed. The mood was one of celebration. So why did she feel like she wanted to cry?

"When's the engagement party?" Jasper asked.

"Two weeks, maybe on the Friday. We want to have it before Jodie leaves."

Hallie's eyes lit up. "Maybe we can make it a joint engagement-farewell."

No. Oh no. Jodie didn't want to be noticed. She intended to quietly slip out of town before anyone could make false promises about keeping in touch or say how much they'd miss her when she knew it wasn't true.

She forced a smile. "No, thank you. I want it to be a happy occasion. Let's focus on you two."

Hallie's smile faded. "If you're sure."

"I'm sure."

———

Brandon knocked on his dad's door.

"Who is it?"

"Just me."

His dad came down the hallway, a blanket in his hands. "How many times do I have to tell you? You don't have to knock."

Brandon pulled a face. "I know. It just takes some getting used to."

Dad grinned, his green eyes so like Brandon's, sparkling in the light. "Get in here and get used to it."

His tone was gruff, but Brandon heard the affection. His hurting heart soaked it up and clung to it like a drowning man. The blanket in his hands moved and Brandon looked closer.

"What have you got?"

"Orphaned squirrel. One of the visitors at the trailer park found it. The mother was dead." His father held the tiny creature up to show him. Covered in a fine layer of fur, it curled up in his dad's hands, eyes closed. Brandon had to admit it was cute.

"What do you feed it?"

"Puppy formula. His name is Edward."

Really? Brandon managed to hide his amusement at the formal name for the tiny creature.

"How was church this morning?" Dad moved down the hallway and placed the squirrel in a box and closed the lid.

Brandon shrugged. "It was okay." He brightened. "You should come with me sometime."

Dad laughed. "I'm the Junk Man, remember?"

"What's that got to do with it? You'd be welcome."

"Pitied, more like it." He turned and walked into the kitchen. "I don't need anyone's pity. Or judgment. I'm happy with my life the way it is."

Brandon followed. His dad was telling the truth. He was happy. The betrayal that had demoted him to the town's Junk Man all those years ago had left him at peace. He was one of the few people Brandon knew who didn't care what people thought of him, didn't strive to get to the top, to own more, be more, have more.

Brandon looked around the living room. "Where's all your geese?" The cages were empty.

Dad smiled. "None in ICU right now. I transferred them to the yard this morning."

"That's good." Brandon grinned then glanced at the table. An official looking letter sat there. "What's this?"

Dad came over and picked it up. "A warning letter from the council." He slapped it against his hand. "They say this place is a breeding ground for snakes and mice. They're going to send someone to inspect my house. Check if it's unsafe or inhabitable."

"What? Why?"

"I'm guessing Susannah Gilbertson's been in their ears going on about my geese. She's probably found someone with influence on council and made it worth their while to hassle me." A look of annoyance passed over Dad's face. "Been here over thirty years and only now is the council complaining they create hygiene issues and noise pollution."

"And you think Susannah's behind it?" Surely she wouldn't resort to such petty tactics.

Dad snorted. "I know she is. Small-town news and all. Rhonda Ingalls thought it was her duty to inform me that Susannah's petitioning to have a new rule limiting how many birds you can keep in town."

Brandon groaned. He should've driven her Lexus down to the lake full of geese. Should've driven it straight in the water. "What'll happen if she finds out you've got a squirrel in here?"

Dad's hand rested on Brandon's shoulder. "It'll be okay, son. Don't you worry about it. You've got enough to worry about. How's your mother?"

Unwanted tears stung his eyes, and frustrated, he blinked them away. "Not too good."

His dad studied him, then sighed. "You keep praying for a miracle. I will, too."

"You've been praying?" Wonder filled Brandon. His father, an unbeliever, would do that for his mother?

Dad shrugged. "Worth a try. Anything's worth a try. Never found much use for prayer myself, but for you ..." He shrugged.

Brandon wished he were game to throw his arms around him, but instead he slapped him on the back. "Thank you."

Dad chuckled awkwardly. "Anything for you, son. Got to make up for lost time."

Yes. Time was the enemy. He'd missed out on time with his father the first twenty-three years of his life. Now, it seemed he'd miss out on time with his mother for the next twenty-three years. And more.

God? Can you hear me? I don't have much family. Please let me keep my mom.

CHAPTER SIX

Jodie filed another book on the college library shelves. Rachel was trialing the receptionist job alone today, so Jodie was helping the librarian with stocktaking.

"I'm too old for this," Lorna Grant said with a groan. She picked up a pile of books and dumped them on the cart.

"For what?"

Lorna sighed, pushing her glasses up her nose. Jodie wanted to laugh. She was the quintessential librarian with her gray hair in a bun, glasses chain around her neck, and a learned, knowing look on her face.

"Hauling books around. Chasing after students who are always pulling books off the shelves then putting them back in the wrong place. To be honest, I wish I could take the admin position you're leaving."

Jodie laughed. "I imagine my pay grade is a bit below yours."

Lorna shook her head. "I don't do this for the pay. I do it because there's a need. And since Graham died …" Her voice faded out and Jodie touched the older woman's shoulder. The whole town had grieved when her husband was killed at work. Lorna was a people person, and Jodie knew she must be lonely.

"So why don't you go for the admin position? Rachel hasn't been given the job yet. Maybe the college can advertise for a new librarian instead." Even as she spoke, an idea was falling into place.

"Librarians don't grow on trees, Jodie. Being a librarian requires a degree in library science. It's a bit more than putting books on shelves." Lorna was still smiling, but Jodie wondered if she'd offended her. Made her feel underestimated or undervalued.

"I know," she said quickly. "My friend Hallie is a librarian, and she's the smartest woman I know." Hallie had been a librarian in Missouri before she began volunteer work here for the church. But she would need a regular, paid job now she was engaged to Josh and staying in Trinity Lakes. Working here would be perfect for her.

She pictured Hallie working in the college library and Josh sneaking in for a kiss behind shelves between classes. She smiled. That would keep Rachel away from them. But were staff allowed to date students? Surely if they were already engaged … Maybe this had been God's plan all along. She needed to speak to Peter as soon as possible. Before he gave Rachel the admin job.

Thankfully Peter was in his office during her lunch hour and able to see her.

"Come in, Jodie," he said with a welcoming smile. His hair was a distinguished gray, his eyes intelligent.

She sat across from him and studied the gold of the "Director Peter Franklin" name plaque on his desk. *Oh God, you know what's best. Please work it all out for good.*

"How can I help?"

Jodie drew in a deep breath. "I know Rachel is trying out for my position, but I have an idea I want to put to you."

Peter steepled his hands, looking amused. "Let's hear it."

"You know Hallie Hollaway, my brother's fiancée? She's a

qualified librarian. She used to work in a library in Springfield before she came here. Her plan was she might return one day, but then Josh…" She shrugged and Peter grinned.

"Josh gave her a reason to stay."

"Exactly. While I was helping Lorna in the library this morning, she mentioned how the work feels a bit much sometimes. She said she wished she could take my position but doesn't want to leave the college without a librarian. So, I was thinking, what about if you offered Lorna my job and offer Hallie the library job? Lorna's such a people person, and my job would put her right in the middle of everything that's going on. She knows how the college works. She'd slot right in."

Peter didn't say anything, but she could see he was contemplating her suggestion. He rubbed his forehead, then swiveled his chair and looked out his office window. Jodie followed his gaze. The view of the lake was beautiful. But she'd looked at it for so many years it didn't bring any joy. She was ready to move on.

"It's worth considering." Peter turned back and picked up a pen before writing something on a piece of paper in front of him. He looked at her again and smiled, his eyes crinkling in the corners. "Will you pray with me about this, bring it before the Lord?"

"Of course." Jodie bowed her head and prayed for God's paths to be made clear. Then Peter prayed, his prayer including God's blessing over Jodie as she moved to New York. Jodie let his prayer wash over her. God was in this. She could feel it. How good was it the way He brought everything together; the way He was in every detail?

———

Jodie arrived home from work to find Hallie at the door, car keys in hand.

"I'm about to go 'round to Josh's," she said. "Want to come?"

Jodie shook her head, then changed her mind. She wouldn't be around much longer, and she needed to make the most of the time she had. "Yeah. I'll get changed." She could finish packing later.

She raced upstairs, past Hallie's room—once Esther's room—and to her own. She pulled on a pair of jeans. Might as well spend some time with Josh and Hallie. She saw Josh a whole lot less now he'd moved into the cottage next to the Junk Man. And even though Hallie lived with them now, she was always off somewhere with Josh.

"I've got him a C-pen." Hallie looked pleased with herself as she drove across town.

"What's a C-pen?"

"A pen that you run along a line of writing and it reads it for you. It will help him with his studies and essay writing."

"I thought he wanted you to help him with his essays." Jodie grinned.

"Yeah, but it hasn't quite worked so well ..." Red crept up into Hallie's cheeks, matching her hair, and Jodie laughed.

"You're too distracting. He can't keep his hands off you, can he?"

Hallie's cheeks looked like they were on fire. "Something like that."

Jodie chuckled. If Hallie was offered the job in the college library, she was going to need to learn not to let Josh distract her.

———

HALLIE PULLED up outside the front of Josh's little cottage, and Jodie looked for Brandon's truck next door. He should be at work, yet she'd hoped he'd be next door, visiting his dad. His dad's vehicle wasn't there either. He was likely still cleaning up along the edge of the lake somewhere. She respected the man for his dedication to keeping the lakefront clean and helping the wildlife. She'd been afraid of the man she'd known as the Junk Man in her childhood years. He still made her uncomfortable with his quiet, reserved ways and gruff demeanor, but his eyes were kind. And now she knew his story, she knew he was a decent man.

Josh opened the door and drew Hallie up into a warm hug and a kiss. It may have gone on longer, but Jodie cleared her throat to remind them she was there.

Hallie pushed back from Josh with a chuckle. "I brought a visitor."

Josh looked around Hallie to grin at Jodie. "That's not a visitor. That's my sister. She's like a piece of old furniture."

"Well, thanks." Jodie pretended to pout as she swatted Josh on the arm and pushed past him into the living room. "That means I can help myself to your stash of choc-chip cookies."

Josh dropped his hands from around Hallie and darted down the hall to the kitchen entrance. "Who says I've got cookies?"

"Who says you're Josh Ladan?"

"What's that mean?" He held up an arm to barricade his kitchen.

"Josh Ladan always has cookies, and I'm going to find them." She ducked under his arm and opened the kitchen cupboard. "Where are they?"

He pulled at her shirt, dragging her back. "Hey, this is my house. If you dare steal my cookies ..."

"But I'm just an old piece of furniture, Josh. If I belong here, it wouldn't be stealing." She spun around to face him and tapped her chin. "However, if you'd like to revise your statement and treat me like an honored guest, I might be polite and not ask for food. Or coffee. Or any of the things a normal host would offer if they had a polite bone in their body."

Josh sputtered, then turned to Hallie. "Are you hearing this?

You brought this … this *guest* into my house to treat me like this?"

"Hello?"

The familiar deep voice at the door had them all turning. Brandon. Jodie's heart gave a leap.

"Brando," Josh said, going to the door. "Come in, mate. It's just like old times in here."

———

BRANDON OPENED the door and walked down the hall into the cottage.

"Old times?"

Jodie peeked around the door with a cheeky grin and waved at him. "Hi, Brandon."

He looked back at Josh who was grinning too.

"Yeah, she's battling me for my chocolate chip cookies, but we'll beat her. Just like old times."

Brandon laughed, remembering the sibling battles he'd become involved in over the years. Of course he'd always sided with Josh, but Jodie never seemed to mind. She appeared to enjoy the challenge.

"What about me?" Hallie's eyes sparkled as she came out from the kitchen. She poked Josh in the side. "Do I not count in this battle?"

"You?" Josh drew her into his arms and kissed her soundly on the lips. "You are worth more than anyone in this room. You are worth a thousand chocolate chip cookies."

Hallie grinned. "Great. So you won't mind that I just gave the packet to your *guest.*"

"What? No!"

Jodie came out of the kitchen and waved the packet provocatively in the air, eyes sparkling.

"Here. Brandon." She tossed them high over Josh's head. Brandon reacted just in time, catching them neatly.

Josh held out his hand, expecting him to pass them over, but Brandon took a step back. He looked from Hallie to Jodie to Josh. Now what? Loyalties had changed. Bringing Hallie into the friendship between him, Josh, and Jodie had changed everything.

Josh continued to look at him expectantly. Hallie was smiling. Jodie's eyes were pleading, hopeful. How could he ignore her when she looked at him that way?

"Sorry, Josh." He pulled a cookie from the packet and bit into it. He sealed it again and tossed the packet back to Jodie. She caught it like the champion she was and gave him a conspiratorial wink. Brandon had to admit it was fun being on her side.

She took out a cookie and licked her lips. "Mm." She eyed the packet, looked at Josh, then licked her lips again. "What can I do to make sure I get to eat the whole packet?"

"Nooo!" Josh called. "Brando, what have you done? She's going to lick them all."

Jodie slowly lowered her head toward the packet, a delightfully mischievous glint in her eyes. Then she ran her tongue along the cookies that poked out the open end of the packet.

Now that was going one step too far. Brandon charged at her at the same time as Josh. Josh wrestled her for the cookie packet while Brandon caught her around the waist to stop her escaping out the back door. Jodie laughed and fought against them. Josh managed to claim the cookie packet while Brandon grabbed her arms and held them firm against her stomach, pulling her back against his chest. He pinned her there and she lay her head back against him, breathing hard. Her hair tickled his nose and she seemed to settle there. Her delightful giggles made him want to spin her around and kiss her.

He dropped her arms and stepped back.

"That was a nice afternoon snack for an old piece of furniture like me," she said, rubbing her stomach.

Hallie stood to the side, laughing, and Josh rolled his eyes. Brandon looked between all three of them and smiled. Just like old times. He missed this. Missed the fun, the laughter, the banter. Some days, he felt like an old man with all the responsibility of caring for his mother. Death was too close, too often on his mind. Childish fun was exactly what he needed to remind him he was still young, still alive.

———

THEY ALL SAT around the table, the packet of chocolate chip cookies in the center. Jodie watched as Brandon took one, stared at her with a challenge in his eyes and then ate it, his gaze never leaving hers. It did things to her heart and left a strange fluttering in her belly. Best to pretend he wasn't there and not look at him at all.

She focused on Hallie and Josh. Hallie presented Josh with his C-pen.

"It's amazing." Josh tried it out on a printed piece of paper and a voice read back the typed text. "Wow. I didn't know these existed."

"We used to have one in the library in Springfield," Hallie said. "We got it for a little boy with low vision, but I'd forgotten about it until a couple of weeks ago."

Josh tried it out again, then looked at Hallie, his eyes alight with love.

"It's perfect. Thank you." He leaned over to give her a kiss.

"At least the C-pen won't be as distracting as having Hallie help you with assignments," Jodie said.

Josh laughed. "You're the distraction. Coming in here, stealing my cookies. You realize I'm going to have to get Hallie to write a note explaining why I couldn't get my assignment done? We had a thief break in. It was very distressing."

"Ha. You invited me in." Jodie's smile widened. "But don't worry. In two weeks, you won't have to put up with me anymore."

Josh looked alarmed. "Two weeks. Wow, that's come up quick."

"Quick? I've been waiting a long time for this." Excitement danced within. "Two weeks feels like forever."

No one spoke.

"Come on, it's a good thing. You should be happy to get rid of me."

"Of course we're happy for you," Hallie said brightly, but it seemed forced. She looked at Josh. "I know we'll miss her, but isn't it great the way God's worked everything out for her? That scholarship was an answer to prayer. God's hand is so clearly in this."

Jodie smiled. God was working everything out for Hallie too, especially if Peter Franklin offered her the job in the college library.

Brandon stood. "Well, my dad is probably home from work now. I'll catch you all later."

Her stomach twisted. That was it? No comment about her leaving? Didn't he care? She watched him walk out the door, giving them all a brief wave.

"Don't let him fool you Jodie," Hallie said as the door clicked shut. "He cares. He just doesn't know how to say it."

"Me either." Josh grinned and threw the empty cookie packet at her. "So take this as my love language."

"Throwing trash?"

"At old furniture. Yes."

Jodie giggled and stood to give him a hug. He always knew how to lighten the mood. "Love you, Josh. I'll miss you."

CHAPTER SEVEN

Lorna met Jodie in the library the following morning with a huge hug.

Jodie chuckled and stepped back. "What was that for?"

Lorna put her hands on either side of Jodie's face. "You, dear, dear girl. Peter told me your idea. He's going to contact your friend the librarian. If she says yes, I'll be able to take your job." She looked around, eyes bright. "You know, I only kept this job for so many years because there was no one else to do it. Or so I thought. But God had it all worked out."

The thought challenged Jodie. Maybe if Lorna had prayed about it and stepped down earlier, God would have provided someone else earlier. "I love that God isn't confined to perceived needs," she said. "He made the whole universe. He knows our needs and created the way to fill them. Like He did through Jesus at the cross."

Lorna looked at her. "You sure you're meant to be a journalist, not a preacher?"

Jodie bit her lip. There she went again. Preaching at people. She didn't even know why she did it. Maybe some subconscious need to prove herself? To show she was worthy of being a Ladan? Or was it a way of keeping people at a distance?

"Now, today we need to move that bookshelf." Lorna pointed to a huge now-empty bookshelf against the side wall of the library. It was made of solid wood and looked centuries old.

Jodie stifled a laugh. Surely Lorna wasn't serious? And yet she appeared to be.

"Why are we moving the bookshelf?"

"Because we have a new projector screen and it needs more space. This wall is bigger. Now if you can swivel that end, I'll let you know when to stop."

Jodie bit her lip, eyeing the huge old piece of furniture. "I don't know that I can do it on my own. How about if I check if Peter's around to help?"

"Yeah. Might be a good idea."

Jodie took a last look at the huge bookshelf and headed to the director's office, chuckling.

"Knock, knock."

Peter Franklin looked up with a smile. "Jodie. How can I help you?"

"Well, you can help save the college an insurance claim by helping me move a huge bookshelf for Lorna."

"She was going to do it?"

Jodie grinned. "No, she was smarter than that. She asked me to."

Peter laughed as he put down the pen he was holding and stood. "In that case, I'll come immediately. You're right. We can do without accidents."

He followed Jodie to the library and his eyes widened when he saw the bookshelf. Then his lips twitched.

"Let's give it a try, shall we?"

Jodie looked at Peter. He wasn't young anymore. Greying and in his sixties, he probably shouldn't be doing this either. She would have asked Josh, but his brain injury left him prone to migraines, so he had to be careful about exerting himself. Dad was here somewhere lecturing today. He was close to Peter's age too, but between the two of them …

"What if I ask Dad to help? I can text him and see if he's free."

Peter's eyes twinkled. "Sounds like a good idea." He glanced at his watch. "Class should have just finished."

Ten minutes later, Dad joined them. He didn't even blink at the size of the bookshelf. He pulled up his sleeves.

"Right. Where do you want it?"

Lorna bit her lip. "Um … I'm not totally sure."

"Well, you'd better decide." Dad laughed. "I don't think we'll be moving it twice."

So he had been at least a little bit intimidated by the size of the thing.

Lorna put her hands on her hips. "Okay. Let's just twist it around against here." She tapped the adjacent wall. "We need this wall for our projector screen."

Peter nodded. "Right. Jodie, you guide that end. Theo, you, and I will shove it from this end."

With a great deal of grunting and heaving, they managed to slide the bookshelf into place.

Dad tapped the side of the shelf. "They don't make them like they used to, do they?"

"Thank the good Lord." Lorna wiped her brow as though she'd been the one moving it, not just watching and directing.

Jodie looked at the place the shelf had been. An old book lay on the bare floor. Its leather cover was worn and cracked. She picked it up.

"What's this?"

Lorna came over and took it from Jodie's hands. "Looks like an old journal." She flipped it open and squinted. "Henry Bellamy. That name rings a bell."

Peter joined them, still breathing hard. "He's the one who

bought this building to use it as a Bible college. It was originally a children's home, back in the late 1800s."

He skimmed through the journal.

"What should we do with it? It looks old." Lorna peered over Peter's shoulder.

"It is. These entries date back to 1915. Listen to this." Peter carefully held the journal open and read aloud.

"Father has suggested I record all my Father in Heaven has done for me. I don't even know where to begin. First, I suppose, I should introduce myself. I am Henry Charles Bellamy, but I was born Henry Dawes. My parents died of influenza when I was two. I still have vague memories of being carted away, screaming for my mother. I was placed in the Trinity Lakes Children's Home. The horrors I experienced there were unspeakable, and I barely survived from one day to the next.

In 1912, Carlisle and Vera Bellamy arrived from Australia. He was a wealthy sheep farmer who had travelled to do research on sheep farming in America. The moment I saw him, I knew he was kind. He had a ready smile and asked me many questions for which I had no answers. Later, he and his wife took me to Australia.

They had told the director they needed an heir to take over their farm one day. But it was more than that—Vera Bellamy was barren, and they had prayed for a child. They adopted me when God whispered in their spirits that I was the one they had prayed to receive. I cannot tell you how blessed I am."'

Peter cleared his throat and Jodie was drawn back to the present. This Henry Bellamy was an integral part of the college's history, but shouldn't his family have his journal? Journals were personal. Hers were, anyway. What was it doing here behind the shelf? Something tugged within, a desire to make sure the journal was returned to its rightful owners and valued as it ought to be. But no. She was leaving. Henry Bellamy left, didn't he? No one stayed in this place. Not for long. She couldn't afford to get involved.

"You said Henry founded this college?" Dad asked.

Peter nodded.

"So what do we do with the journal? Who has the right to it?"

Jodie's question exactly.

Peter frowned. "I don't know. It was found here, but I feel as though this kind of history belongs to everybody." His eyes lit up. "I'll ask Ellie Reilly. She might like a copy for the museum. She's doing a great job with the reopening. Olivia Darcy knew what she was doing, giving her the manager's position. I'd trust Ellie to know its value."

"What about Henry's family?" Jodie didn't want to get involved, but she felt compelled to ask.

"We need to follow up with them."

Everything within Jodie wanted to offer to do it. But Lorna winked at her, then turned to Peter, her eyes dancing with excitement.

"If everything goes to plan, I'll soon have the time to do it."

Peter's lips twitched at Lorna's poor attempt at being discreet. "How about we go into my office and make a plan."

Jodie watched them leave, then looked up at Dad's puzzled expression.

"What's that about?"

Jodie grinned. "I think our prayers for a full-time job for Hallie will soon be answered."

"BRANDON, HAVE YOU SEEN THIS?"

Brandon put down his wrench. Bruce held a poster in his hands and Brandon leaned over to look.

Surprise and dismay hit him in equal measure. "That's my dad's house." He read the words splashed across the image.

DEMOLISH THIS INFESTED EYESORE

PROTECT OUR TOWN

He groaned. "Susannah Gilbertson. She's even had rubbish photoshopped into the front yard. She should know better than to poke the bear."

"You think it was her?" Bruce looked surprised. "It was some young kid who asked me to put it in our window."

"Susannah's smart enough not to do her own dirty work, but she's not smart enough to know that the more she tries to push my dad, the more he'll dig his heels in."

Bruce frowned. "What exactly does she have against your dad?"

"It's something that happened in the past." Brandon measured his words. "A relative of hers did something less than aboveboard and she thinks it might affect her if it gets out. My dad was wronged. Now that some people have figured it out, she's getting scared. She wants to scare him into silence."

"That's low."

Brandon nodded. "The crazy thing is, Dad would've kept quiet if she'd left him alone. Instead she came to his house last year, screeched at him and demanded he keep quiet, then she gouged his cheek with her diamond ring. He ended up having stitches."

"Seriously?" Bruce shook his head and screwed the poster in his hands into a tight ball. "I hope he sued the ... well, I hope he sued her."

"No. Dad might be stubborn, but he doesn't fight if he doesn't have to. Although maybe he should have."

"Well, I'm not having anything to do with that crazy woman and her schemes." Bruce's look turned thoughtful. "Isn't she a churchie, like you?"

"Yeah." Brandon grunted. "But just because someone goes to church doesn't mean we live the way we should. We're all human."

"I don't know. Some humans act more like animals." Bruce tossed the ball of paper toward the garbage can.

"Don't let my dad hear you saying that." Brandon grinned. "He tells me animals are way more trustworthy than humans. At least you know which ones to trust and which ones to avoid."

Bruce chuckled. "He could have a good point there. Well, let me know if I can do anything to help. I'm too scared of that woman to put myself directly in the line of fire, but if there's anything I can do behind the scenes … you know what I mean."

Brandon laughed. He knew exactly what Bruce meant.

"I'm not too scared to admit I'm a coward," Bruce said with a wink as he headed back to the ride-on lawn mower he'd been fixing for the local Bible college.

"That's not being a coward. That's knowing when it's worth the risk or not. I call that wisdom."

"Ha." Bruce let out a burst of laughter. "If you say so. I knew I kept you around for a reason. Someone has to know the real reason I do the things I do."

"Or the things you don't do."

Bruce turned and looked back. "Sometimes I think your talents are wasted here, Brandon. You're too smart for this job." He pointed a work worn finger at Brandon. "But don't listen to me. I'm happy for you to waste away in here for my benefit."

CHAPTER EIGHT

"I'm starting a new job in two weeks," Hallie announced at dinner. She smiled around the table, eyes shining with excitement. "Peter Franklin asked me to be the new librarian at the Bible college." She looked at Jodie. "I believe it's you I need to thank."

Jodie grinned. "No, I think God gave me the idea. Lorna told me she was feeling overwhelmed in the library, and the thought just hit me. It makes so much sense."

"It will be full-time," Hallie said almost apologetically, looking at Mom and Dad. "I won't be able to do as much as I've been doing for the church."

Mom reached across to touch her hand. "We knew your volunteer work at church and for the Brown family was just for a season. I had thought a few weeks. Nine months is more than any of us ever expected."

Hallie drew in a breath. "I still feel bad. Abella cried when I told her."

"What about Madison?" Jodie pictured the sunny little girl Hallie cared for after school.

"All sorted." Hallie smiled again as she picked up her piece of bread and neatly buttered it. "Peter asked me to run a weekday homework club and playgroup for kids of students in the library. It gives the parents a chance to study or do their assignments undisturbed. He's happy for Madison to join them."

"What does her mom think about that?" As far as Jodie knew, Madison's mother still had doubts about God.

"She loves the idea of Maddie being around other kids. She doesn't seem to mind the Christian influence." Hallie placed her butter knife across her plate and picked up a piece of bread, taking a delicate bite.

Jodie watched in fascination. Hallie Hollaway had to be the tidiest person she knew. Josh was the complete opposite, but at least he made an effort for Hallie.

She folded a slice of bread and bit into it. Much easier. And quicker.

"Looks like it's all coming together," she said with a grin around her mouthful.

"Yes." Mom looked delighted. "And in other good news, I got a call from Esther today. She's coming home for the engagement party. She's bringing Mark as well."

She was? Jodie fought the hurt that slashed across her chest. When she'd told Esther she was leaving for New York and invited her home for a last sisterly catch up, Esther said she was too busy with school. It hadn't seemed to matter they'd be so far apart. Not that distance seemed to make any difference. Esther rarely came home anyway. And that conversation had been as short as all their recent conversations. Jodie felt as though she'd lost her sister, her closest friend, and confidante in her growing up years. The bubbly wise and compassionate older sister Jodie had turned to whenever she needed someone to talk to was gone. She'd left. Just like everybody else.

———

JODIE PLACED a pile of books in the packing box. It was a beautiful Saturday morning. She looked around her room. Excitement danced within. Moving day was coming up fast.

She took another book from her shelf. *Koala Lou* by Mem Fox. Grandma had sent it from Australia for her fourth birthday. She had memories of snuggling up to Dad as he read her the story almost every night for years. She blinked. She'd loved leaning against his chest, listening to his deep voice rumble in her ear. Where had her childhood gone? She fondly fingered the pages of the book and swallowed hard.

Feet sounded on the stairs and she looked up. Brandon stood in the doorway, still wearing his work clothes. Her mouth went dry. It wasn't fair that he always looked so good. Her eyes went from his trademark half-smile to his green eyes.

"Brandon." The book fell from her hands. Embarrassed, she bent to retrieve it, dropped it again.

Brandon chuckled, came into her room, and picked it up. "Are you remembering my noble deed of saving you from Mr. Wolf, or are you flustered by my presence?"

Both, but she wasn't going to admit it. "Thanks." She accepted the book from his hand.

"*Koala Lou*? You think you need that for college?" He sounded amused, but it took only one look to see he wasn't making fun of her. This time.

"It might help me with one of my essays. You never know."

He raised an eyebrow. "I suppose it might look good in a bibliography."

Jodie laughed and pushed a strand of blonde hair from her eye. It stubbornly fell back, so she pulled out the band around her ponytail and retied her hair, aware his eyes remained on her.

He took the chair at her desk and straddled it, resting his elbows on the back, his chin in his hands. "I was hoping you could help me with something."

"Oh?" She couldn't remember the last time he'd asked something from her.

"It's more for my dad, really." He looked at his feet then back up again to meet her gaze. "Susannah's trying to get the town onside to demolish Dad's house. She has more money than I do, but she doesn't have as many friends. Especially not friends with the gifts and talents mine have." His look was meaningful.

She waited, not sure what he was getting at.

He frowned, suddenly looking uncertain. "We are friends, aren't we?"

"Of course." Despite having to guard her heart against wishing for more. She blushed.

"Good. I know Josh and I are best friends, but it was your whole family who took me in, filled that missing part of my life."

She swallowed hard, emotion clogging her throat. He said that now, but he'd forget about her in a few weeks. Out of sight, out of mind. "So what can I do for you?"

"I need you to use your investigative journalism skills and do some skulking around before you go."

"Skulking?" She giggled.

"What? You don't think you're capable of skulking?" He grinned then sobered. "Then I need you to write an article for Selena at the Trinity Lakes Gazette showing why Susannah Gilbertson has ulterior motives and what an asset my dad is to this town."

Jodie blinked. She hadn't expected that. She'd written a couple of articles for the Bible college in the past, but nothing like this.

"If we told her what my mom confessed to she'd back down, but I don't want to do that in case she hassles Mom."

Jodie understood completely. If anyone got wind of how Brandon's mom had been involved in a sketchy deal that caused the lakefront to be wrongly zoned twenty-plus years ago, she wouldn't be left alone. The town would be in uproar, and Mariah would be hounded and questioned mercilessly.

"I would pay you," Brandon said.

"No, no. I wouldn't expect that. It'd be a great human-interest story. It's just I don't know how much I can find out before I leave."

"You'll be at church on Sunday, at the engagement party, around town. You can talk to the women around town. They talk more than guys do. They know more."

"You're such a genderist."

His green eyes lit up. "So you'll do it?"

"What?" She laughed loudly. "How did you get that from me calling you a name?"

He grinned. "It shows you love me."

What? Why did her heart beat crazily at his words, his look? He meant it in a friend-love kind of way. That was all.

He dropped his chin from his hands, his expression turning serious. "I know you'll be busy. I guess I just hope you'll hear something or think of something. I totally understand if you don't, but I wanted to put the idea out there."

"I'll do my best." For him, she'd do anything. Especially when he looked at her that way.

"Thanks. You're a gem." He grinned at her. "Don't let anybody tell you otherwise."

She watched as he bounded back down the stairs. Since when was Brandon Taylor so warm and encouraging? He had no right to come in here and try to worm his way into her heart. She wasn't going to let him. No way.

CHAPTER NINE

Jodie looked up as a teenager walked in the door of the Bible college office. She gave him her most friendly smile. Only one week to go. She was spending half her remaining time at the reception desk, and half in the library. Hallie was coming in during the afternoons to get a feel for the place. Maddie always came with her, bouncing along and chattering nonstop.

"Hello. I have something I'd like to hang up around campus," the teenager said. "It's for the benefit of our town, an attempt to keep the heart of our community."

Jodie saw the pile of posters in his hand, caught a glimpse of the image on the front. "Whose house is that?"

"The Junk Man's." The teenager puffed out his chest. "We're starting a petition to have his house demolished—"

"Can I see?" Jodie darted around from behind the reception desk and took the pile. Anger heated her chest as she read the poster. Someone had added junk to the front yard that she knew for a fact wasn't there. They'd also made the house look more dilapidated than it was. "Who made these posters?"

The teenager shuffled his feet. "Ah, I can't say."

Susannah Gilbertson, no doubt. She looked at the teenager and felt sorry for him. "What's your name?"

"Kynan."

"Kynan. I know you're just doing a job, but the information on these posters simply isn't true. Luke's house is not infested."

"The Junk Man?"

"Yes. That's his real name. Luke McAffrey. He's a qualified environmental planning officer and he's doing our community a great service by caring for our wildlife. He keeps our lakefront clean."

Kynan's eyes were wide. "But—"

"I know Susannah said otherwise, but even this picture has been photoshopped. Can you see here, where the trash is the wrong shape and the edge is blurred? That's where someone cut and pasted a picture of trash and put it over a picture of his house."

Kynan paled. "Um, I didn't know."

"I believe you. But now you do know, would you be willing to tell me about these posters? Like who made them? Who's paying you to take them around town?"

Kynan backed toward the door. "It's just a job. That's all."

Then he turned and ran.

Jodie sighed. Well, that hadn't gone well. She hadn't learned half the information she wanted to. If she had spare time she'd definitely be doing more "skulking" for Brandon and his dad. Susannah Gilbertson was a menace.

Lord, you know I don't have time to help with this, so please send the right people. Please protect Brandon's father and bring about justice.

Hallie walked in, Maddie dancing at her heels. Not the right time to tell her what had happened. Hallie looked excited.

"Did Peter tell you about the journal they found in the library?"

"Yes, I've seen it." Jodie smiled at the memory. "What are they going to do with it?"

"Lorna and I will follow it up." Hallie beamed. "I get to trace the family history and see if I can find any living relatives. Who would have imagined I'd get paid to do what I love again?"

Jodie laughed. "A bit like Ellie Reilly in the museum. You two are a pair, with your love of history."

"So long as it comes in book form. I don't much care for old dresses and furniture and mouse-infested relics."

"I doubt Ellie would let mice in the museum."

"No." Hallie shuddered. "But some of those old things still smell musty."

"And books don't?"

"No. They don't." Hallie looked appalled at the suggestion. "Old books have a unique smell. It's the smell of memories. Of mystery and stories of people of the past who held the book and delved into another world that only those who read the book can share."

"Yeah, and those who didn't wash their hands so it smells of dirt and grease and I wouldn't like to name what else."

"Jodie." Hallie tried to look horrified, but her eyes twinkled.

Jodie went back to the pile of books she was shelving. "How about you keep your old books, and I'll go off to New York and maybe write my own book one day."

Hallie laughed. "You do that."

————

BRANDON WAS FUMING. More and more posters were showing up around town, and somebody had begun dumping trash in his father's yard. He stalked past it, anger burning a fire in his chest.

"Dad?" He walked in the door and Dad came to meet him, Edward the squirrel poking his nose out from the zipper in his jacket. "Who did this?" Brandon waved a hand at the mess in the yard.

Dad shrugged. "Susannah's henchman, or maybe people who believe her lies. Who knows?"

"It has to stop."

"Yeah, I've told the sheriff." Dad sighed. "Not that it will do much good. It's like stopping a snowball rolling down a hill, gathering more snow as it gains speed."

Brandon frowned, not liking the picture. He shook his head. "But we have the God who made the snow on our side."

"Hmm."

"We do." Brandon's heart sank at the doubt in his father's eyes. "God is all for truth and justice."

Dad stroked Edward's ears absently. "I could fight this and could probably win, but it's hardly worth it. It'll just keep coming up again."

Brandon sighed, then looked back out the front door at the sound of thumping and clanging. He charged outside.

Josh and Hallie were there with gloves on, picking up rubbish and dumping it into the back of Hallie's truck. They stopped and looked up when Brandon and his dad came down the steps.

"We have to fight for justice," Hallie said, a deep furrow in her brow. Her red hair glistened in the sunlight and she looked as fiery as Brandon felt.

"That's right." Josh picked up an old sheet of tin and threw it into the back of the truck. "One of my college assignments is about how we can live out Micah 6:8 in a practical way. Do justly, love mercy, walk humbly with our God. And there are all these other great verses, like in Zechariah seven. We're expected to show compassion and administer justice. God calls His people to not abandon the fatherless, the stranger, or the poor."

Brandon felt his father stiffen behind him.

"Dad's not poor," he said, before his father could speak.

"Maybe not," Hallie said. "But he's been victimized for years just because he's different."

And he's fatherless.

Brandon knew how that felt. He'd been fatherless for years. Yes, Dad needed the same Heavenly Father he had found.

Lord, help Dad to receive help. Please let him accept your help, your love. Please become his Heavenly Father.

"Well," Dad said, coming down the steps, Edward still poking out of his jacket. "Someone's soaking up their studies."

Josh looked uncomfortable.

"He's doing so well," Hallie said, pride in her voice and eyes.

"I do appreciate what you're doing," Dad said, and glanced at Brandon. "And even if God doesn't perform the miracle of stopping the snowball, he's brought me friends like you and that's enough."

Was it? Brandon looked around him. Having friends couldn't save a house, could it? Or could it?

Jodie hadn't found anything to help his dad, and he understood. He really did. She was focused on her life in New York. It was as though she'd already gone. But maybe he and his dad would have enough friends left that they could, with God's help, beat this thing.

"I'll grab some gloves and put Edward back in his box." Dad ducked back inside.

"Got a spare pair for me?" Brandon called after him.

Dad lifted his hand in acknowledgment and bounded up the steps back inside.

Hallie looked at Brandon. "What's in his shirt?"

"That's Edward." He laughed at Hallie's look. "A squirrel he's looking after, but perhaps you'd better keep that quiet."

Hallie smiled. "Of course." Then she glanced at Josh. "Bandit's great, but what do you think about getting a squirrel?"

Josh snorted and dragged another piece of tin from the pile.

Brandon grinned at Hallie. "I think that's a no."

CHAPTER TEN

Brandon eyed the crowd in the church hall. Engagement parties were not his thing. He was only here to support his best friend. He'd accepted the honor of being Josh's best man, which meant he was expected to be here, but he didn't feel like socializing. Mom's latest tests revealed the cancer was doing its worst. And Dad was still being slandered around town.

The room buzzed with hyped and happy people, most of them talking about the Anzac Day celebrations taking place tomorrow. Trinity Lakes had so many Australian and New Zealanders that they'd brought the Australasian celebration of Anzac Day with them, including an Australian football match.

He could hear Josh trash-talking the US team members even though he wasn't allowed to play because of his brain injury. Josh made up for it by supporting the Aussie/New Zealand team whole-heartedly. The laughter and banter grated against Brandon's somber mood.

He sighed. He didn't need to bring his sadness into that space. He slipped into the kitchen, managing to avoid talking to anyone. Jodie was setting out cups, her back to him.

He came up behind her. "Looks like you and I had the same idea."

She turned to look at him. "What's that?"

"Hiding out in the kitchen."

"I'm helping."

And there was that superior tone and look again. The wall she so often put in place. Well, he wasn't going to let her push him away tonight. It might be the last time he saw her for a long time. As much as they bickered, she'd been like family to him these past five years.

"What can I do to help?"

She didn't even glance up. "Nothing. I've got it under control."

He watched her back for a few moments then straightened his shoulders. She couldn't stop him helping.

He picked up the coffee pot on the counter. "Where do I fill this?"

She sighed, seeming to realize he wasn't going to leave. "The dispenser."

Brandon turned to the hot water dispenser and stared at it. How did the water come out? Should he turn this little spigot? Or push it in. Or pull it out? Tentatively he pushed. The water gushed out, filling the pot.

He set it down and watched Jodie again. She was busy setting out the sugar and teaspoons. Avoiding him.

Why? What made her shut him out? She was leaving in a few days. Surely she could talk to him. Or was she hurting as much as he was? Josh had told him Esther was supposed to come but had pulled out at the last minute. Was that the issue? He'd noticed how sensitive Jodie was about the fact her sister no longer stayed in touch.

He put the pot down and Jodie grabbed it.

"That doesn't go there." She moved it onto a hot mat across the other side of the counter.

With a shrug, Brandon searched through the pile of party items for some plastic cups. It wasn't summer yet, but some people might want cold drinks. He found the cups and ripped them out of their plastic packaging. Then he set them up, one by one beside the coffee cups.

"They have to go over this side." Jodie's voice came from beside him. She reached across and slid the cups to the other side of the counter.

Brandon frowned. "I'm sure there's no rules."

Jodie stopped and her blue eyes met his for the first time. "No, but there are children here. If the plastic cups are near the hot drinks, we're more likely to have children under the adults' feet. We don't want anyone getting burned."

"Oh." Brandon glanced out at the group now playing a game Jasper had come up with. Jodie was right. A few children, including Madison and the Brown children were among the guests cheering as Jasper encouraged them to pile toilet paper on top of Hallie's head in the form of a veil. Poor Hallie looked embarrassed, her cheeks the same shade of red as her hair. The group then began making a suit for Josh out of aluminum foil.

Brandon shook his head and moved the rest of the plastic cups to the position Jodie had suggested.

Finally finished, he stood beside Jodie, watching through the servery window. Everyone clapped and cheered at the ridiculous-looking couple. Josh bent down and kissed Hallie, and the foil tore as he moved.

Brandon glanced at Jodie. She stared straight ahead. The silence between them was awkward. If only Jasper would hurry up and end the game so they could bring out refreshments.

But Theo Ladan clapped for attention and began to make a speech. With a huff, Brandon went to the cups. Might as well fill them.

"We can't do that," Jodie said.

Brandon was tired of feeling inferior and ignorant. Irritation welled up. "We can."

Jodie turned on him, rolling her eyes. "We can, if we want everyone to have cold coffee."

"Your dad won't be long."

"You don't know that."

Brandon continued filling cups.

"Brandon!"

Now she was being childish. He ignored her fierce whisper.

"Stop it," she hissed and grabbed his arm. Hot water splashed across his shirt, burning his skin for the briefest of moments before he pulled his shirt away from his chest.

Jodie gasped, eyes wide with horror. "Quick, we have to put cool water on it."

It seemed she really did care about him, as much as she pretended otherwise.

Before he could tell her he was okay, she was undoing his shirt buttons. Then she stood staring at his bare chest devoid of any kind of mark let alone a burn. Slowly she stepped back, her face flaming red. When she managed to look at him, she looked as stunned as he felt.

Slowly, amusement took over. He couldn't help the smile that curled his mouth.

"Keep going. You've only half undressed me." Immediately he regretted his words. She twisted on her heel to leave, but not before he saw her look of total remorse and revulsion.

He grabbed her arm. "Jodie, wait. Please."

She froze. Finally she turned and looked up at him. His heart hurt to see the tears glistening in her eyes.

He swallowed hard. "I'm sorry, I shouldn't have said that. But … I just don't understand why you're upset with me all the time."

She didn't answer. She was still staring at his chest as though she couldn't look away. He did up his buttons.

"You haven't done anything, not really," she finally whispered.

"Then why are you acting like this? Shutting me out?"

She looked away, cleared her throat. "Oh look, they're ready."

She was right. People were coming to the counter for refreshments.

"What happened to your shirt, Brandon?" Rachel asked as she peered through the servery window.

He shrugged. "Jodes and I had a bit of a biffo. She won."

Jodie kept her head down but a smile tipped the corners of her mouth.

"A biffo?" Rachel looked confused. Biffo was an Aussie word Josh used to refer to a scuffle or disagreement, but Brandon wasn't going to explain. He'd finally made Jodie smile, and that's what mattered.

JODIE'S CONFUSION WAS OVERWHELMING. She'd tried to ignore Brandon tonight, to not feel anything, to not let him get under her skin, but she'd failed spectacularly. She'd been unreasonably snippy. And when she thought she'd hurt him ...

She didn't want this to be her last memory of him before she left.

"You gonna pass me those plates anytime soon?"

She glanced up, her eye catching the tendons moving in his forearms as he ran the dish brush over another plate. His sleeves were rolled up to his elbows and his hands looked almost clean.

"Any slower and you'd be an old church hymn," he said with a grin.

A smile escaped. She passed him the stack of plates. His fingers brushed hers and the awareness that shot through her was disturbing.

Heat filled her cheeks. That was twice she'd touched him in one night. Her own unwritten rule was never to touch him. Never let him think she was interested, trying to get his attention.

"I'm sorry Esther didn't come," he said.

Her throat closed up. She picked up a dish towel. Dared to look at him again.

His intense gaze met hers. "Is that why you're hiding in the kitchen instead of saying goodbye to everyone?"

Heat filled her chest. "I'm not—" Well, yes, she was. She bit her lip. "I don't like goodbyes."

He put down the dish brush and leaned against the counter. "And yet you're leaving."

"It's easier this way." She focused on wiping each individual drip off the plate in her hands.

"Easier for who?"

"Easier for whom."

His eyes widened and he shook his head. "Why do you always do that?"

"Do what?"

"Treat me like some little kid who needs correcting. Is that the best defense mechanism you've got?"

"I'm not being defensive." And yet she knew her body language shouted defensiveness. She deliberately relaxed her shoulders and swallowed the lump in her throat.

Lord, help me. Please. Truth wrestled with reason. She couldn't admit that she'd miss Brandon. Admit that deep down she wanted him to miss her, too. She'd thought she was past this. Past caring. Past being hurt.

"Why do you shut everyone out?" he asked. "Why don't you let anyone close?"

"I'm close to my family." Yep. Still defensive.

He tilted his head and just looked at her. Those green eyes

had always done something to her heart. It was like they looked right through her. He was way too good-looking for his own—for her own—good.

She sighed. If he wanted the truth, she'd tell him. At least some of it. "I've had to let go of people my whole life," she said. "When I was little, Dad worked full-time at the Bible College, and we lived in the on-campus staff housing. New students came every year, and I'd make friends with their kids. Then they'd leave. Sometimes within a year, sometimes after three years. The ones who left after three years were the worst." She swallowed hard and twisted the dish towel in her hands. "Like Hallie. She and her family left to go overseas, and I thought I'd never see her again."

Brandon took the dish towel from her hands and set it on the countertop. "But she came back."

"She nearly didn't."

He frowned. "What do you mean?"

Should she tell him? She wanted to. Wanted to prove she had reason to fear. "She was attacked on the island where her family were missionaries. A man was going to kill her. That's why her family came back to the States."

Brandon's eyes widened. "No way."

"That's why I went off at you that time you messed with her heart and pretended to have feelings for her. She's been through enough."

Brandon's eyes narrowed. "That was ages ago. Before she was with Josh. And I said I was sorry. I made amends. For a pastor's daughter, you're not very good at forgiving and forgetting, are you?"

He was right, but she'd needed to remind herself why he was not someone she could let close. Not someone she could fall for. "That's not actually biblical," she said. "Forgiving doesn't mean forgetting."

Brandon rubbed a hand across his face. Then he sighed, a defeated sound.

Silence fell as they continued their rhythm of washing and drying. "You know," he said quietly, turning to her, "I think we all fear goodbyes to some extent."

Her heart pounded. What was he saying? That he didn't want her to go? That he'd miss her? She hadn't realized how desperately she'd wanted him to say it.

He cleared his throat. "My grandfather died suddenly, and I think that's the worst kind of goodbye."

Confusion swirled around her heart and mind. It was awful that he'd lost his grandfather, but was he minimizing the loss she'd felt when people had left? Comparing them, saying they were lesser because they weren't actually deaths?

"He was the one who encouraged my love of cars, of racing." He rubbed at a rough spot on his knuckles. "It connected us. Made me feel like I belonged. He took me to the Portland International Raceway for my seventh birthday. Up until then, I thought he didn't even like me."

Jodie's mind went back to what she knew about Brandon. He'd had a rough childhood. But this was the first time he'd ever shared any of it with her.

"Sounds like your grandfather wasn't the best role model," she said. "Sometimes there are generational patterns that need to be broken."

He reeled back. She'd hurt him. She could see it in his eyes.

He shook his head and his eyes flashed. "You know, you're not perfect either. I've been here, trying to connect with you all night and you just keep shoving it back in my face. You're so focused on protecting yourself against loss that you don't notice anybody else except to criticize them. But I get it. You can't listen or love when you don't care about anybody except yourself."

Jodie gasped, hurt slashing her chest. How could he think that? She blinked back tears.

He exhaled and shook his head, rubbing the back of his neck. Then he picked up his phone and his wallet and looked back at her. "Good luck, Jodie. You keep protecting that heart of yours, okay? Goodbye."

CHAPTER ELEVEN

A heavy weight filled Brandon's chest as he started his engine. That was the worst goodbye he'd ever experienced.

A knock came at his window, then the door was wrenched open. Jodie stood there.

"Is that how you say goodbye?" Her fingers clenched, then she released them. "I can't believe you'd speak to me like that. Especially when I've just told you how much I hate goodbyes."

She was blaming it on him? His jaw tightened. "You hate goodbyes?" He snorted. "Well, news flash, so do I. I'm experiencing one every day, watching my mom slowly waste away. She's so thin and frail, her bones are poking through her skin. Every breath is an effort. You have no idea how much it hurts to be losing her, but I have to hide it from her because she's already going through enough. But you haven't asked me how she's doing, have you? No, because that might make you care and you're too self-protective to allow yourself to care. You're too scared of loss."

Her mouth sagged, but anger pushed him on. He thumped the steering wheel. "And forgiveness? You think I don't know what it means to forgive? My mom betrayed my trust, Jodie. She lied to me for years. But I still love her. I still pray for a miracle, that God will heal her. You know why? Forgiveness is love. But I don't think you've allowed yourself to love anyone—except your own family, because they're safe. You're so worried about getting hurt that you won't let anyone in."

"Oh really?" Jodie drew up and pointed a shaking finger at him. "You think loving my family is safe? I saw my brother tackled to the ground in some outback town in Australia. I saw him having a fit, coughing up blood. I watched as he was carted off to the hospital, placed into a coma, and then I had to come back to the States for school, not knowing if I'd ever see him alive again. And that same year, my sister left. I faced it all alone."

Brandon let out a scoffing noise. "Alone? You wouldn't know what it's like to be alone if it bit you in the … well, you know. Your parents have always been there for you. And your brother didn't die. Your friend Hallie came back. You have so much, and you can't see it."

"Are you kidding me?" Jodie slapped the top of his door. "The moment Josh came home, you stepped in. *You* changed him. He went from a young man with dreams and potential to a sloth who sat in the basement playing Nascar video games, thinking it was real life. He turned into someone like you, someone who mocked, belittled, and laughed at everyone in the world who wasn't them. Is it any wonder I shut you out? That I learned to guard my heart?"

It was true he'd mocked and belittled people, but he'd also been there for Josh, been a friend and supported him as he dealt with his brain injury. That counted for something, didn't it? And when he'd found out he'd been mocking and belittling his own father without realizing it … something had shifted inside him.

"You talk about forgiveness." He bit back the word on his

tongue. "You don't let anyone change, do you? No, because that would make you feel less spiritual, less important. You put up this façade of being the good little pastor's daughter, but your heart is hard. Your brother needed support. Friendship. Encouragement. I gave him that. I wasn't too wrapped up in my own pain to give it. I helped him live again."

"You think you helped him? I feared for his life every time he got into the car with you. You think you're some racing hero, but you put the lives of people I love in danger every time you get into your truck. Maybe you feel a connection with your grandpa when you speed, but were you listening to my dad's message on Sunday about obeying the rulers and authorities God has placed over us?"

Heat burned like fire in Brandon's chest. He should have known better than to share his heart with her. Should have known she'd tread on what was precious to him. "Preaching does not become you, Jodie. Your dad might be gifted at it, but you're not. You're a condescending little know-it-all. At least your dad cares."

Jodie gasped. Her blue eyes widened and welled up. His heart hurt.

"Let go of my door, Jodie. I need to get home."

"No." Her eyes glistened in the dark. "Not before we sort this out. I'm not going to let the sun go down on my anger."

He stared at her, incredulous. "The sun's long gone. You've already judged me. Nothing I say is going to help. You just throw everything back in my face."

Tears were now streaming down her cheeks. "Please, Brandon ..."

His throat felt red and raw, as did his heart. "What do you want me to say? I don't even know why you're still here. We both know I'm never going to be good enough for you. The son of two outcasts is never going to deserve the pretty, virtuous pastor's daughter."

And that was the absolute truth. Tears stung the back of his throat. He had to get home before he lost it.

"Goodbye, Jodie." In one lightning move he slammed the door shut and reversed the car at the same time.

It took a millisecond to register the thump and the heart-wrenching scream unlike any he'd ever heard before. A wretched sound that stopped his heart as he slammed on the brakes.

Jodie?

Oh God, what had he done? With shaking hands he shoved his door open. Jodie lay on the gravel, face contorted in agony. And then he saw her hand. A mangled mess of fingers. The terrible truth hit him. He'd shut them in his door. He fell to his knees beside her. "Jodie. Jodie, show me."

She doubled over, sounding like she was struggling for breath. Her cries were like a knife stabbing, tearing deep inside him.

"God! Help!" He ran to the door of the hall. Saw someone, unable to process who. "Jodie's been hurt. It's bad. Get help!"

Then he charged back outside, the sound of Jodie's strangled cries of agony hammering pistons through his heart. Footsteps pounded toward them. Josh was there first, followed by his dad.

"What happened?" Josh demanded, punching 911 into his phone.

"I think she got her hand caught in my door."

Why couldn't he say it? That he'd done it? That he'd slammed his door shut on her fingers and reversed the car at the same time? The car must have only moved an inch, but he knew it was enough to tear her fingers and break the bones.

Jodie's father pulled his daughter against his chest and held her while Jocelyn, a paramedic and friend of Hallie's, stemmed the flow of blood from her fingers. He caught a glimpse of the bone poking through. She cried out and Brandon shut his eyes, teeth clenched so hard he tasted blood. How would Theo Ladan ever forgive him for doing this to his daughter? How would he ever forgive himself?

An ambulance arrived and Brandon stood back, unable to look away from the scene unfolding before his eyes. Jocelyn spoke to the paramedics in medical terms he couldn't understand, but he heard words like "compound fracture" and "torn" and "need to save her fingers."

Finally the ambulance left with Jodie and her father, her mother Lil following behind in the car. Then Josh turned to look at him.

"What happened?" His words came out strained.

Brandon couldn't speak. Swallowed. Then he vomited onto the ground.

"It was an accident." Hallie put a hand on his shoulder. He didn't deserve her sympathy. "It's going to be okay."

Going to be okay.

The same words Josh had spoken to him when he'd found out his mother had cancer, that his father was the Junk Man he'd ridiculed his whole life. Well, it wasn't going to be okay. Because those other things had happened to him. But this? This was his doing.

He stared at the blood now drying on the side of his open truck door. He couldn't look away.

"You got any tissues?" Hallie asked.

"In the back seat."

She went around to the other side, found the tissues, and wiped the blood from his door.

Why did she have to be so nice to him? As though wiping away the blood would wipe away the guilt. He looked down at his grease-stained hands. There should be blood on them. Because the honest truth was, he now had blood on his hands.

His phone rang. Mom. She would be wondering where he was. "I ... I need to go home. Let me know ..."

Josh nodded. "I'll call you."

Without another word he climbed into his truck and slowly, slowly drove away, unable to look out his side window, unable to shake the horrible image of Jodie's face screwed up in agony, the heart-wrenching sound of her cries.

He drove home carefully, feeling as though he were in an alternate universe. Nausea swirled in his stomach. He wanted to go to the hospital, check that Jodie was okay, but he wouldn't be welcome. It was torture not knowing exactly how hurt she was. One thing he did know. It was bad.

"Mom?" He came inside, the weight on his shoulders and in his heart too heavy a load to walk tall. He glanced at Mom's nurse and nodded to her, indicating she was free to go now he was here. He still didn't understand how Mom could afford a private nurse, but she'd told him not to worry about it.

He found Mom in the living room on the couch, the tube in her nose feeding her oxygen, the morphine attached to a machine at her side.

"Oh, you're back. I tried to call …" Concern furrowed her brow as she focused on him. "What's wrong? You look awful."

"Mom, I've done something terrible."

She looked at him, eyes sunken and hollow.

He fell onto the couch beside her. "I shut Jodie's hand in my car door."

Mom almost smiled. "She'll forgive you." She drew in a raspy breath. "That girl loves you. I've seen it in her eyes."

What? "No, Mom, she's hurt bad. Might even lose some fingers." He shook his head, wiping his burning eyes. "I should've checked where her hand was. I was just so angry. She was tearing me and Grandpa down, but I should've looked."

"Oh." Mom didn't try to reassure him this time.

He dropped his head into his hands. "Why do we always mess up so much, Mom? What makes us such complete screwups?"

"Hey." Mom put a frail, trembling hand on his shoulder. "We

all mess up, remember? Every single one of us." She leaned her head back against the cushions. "That's why Jesus came. That's what you told me. Do you believe it or not?"

Brandon looked into her eyes dulled with pain. "I believe it." He had to. For his mother's sake. For his own sake. It was his last hope. In his head he knew it was true, but his heart was another matter.

It was true God had forgiven him many years ago when he'd asked Him to.

But what about now? What could be worse than a Christian accepting God's forgiveness but abusing it? He'd used the new life God had given him to enjoy his car and his freedom. He'd used it for himself. And now his carelessness could have scarred Jodie Ladan for life because God had been using her to try to get through to him.

———

Jodie blinked, then blinked again. Where was she?

A woman dressed in blue scrubs came to her side. "Hello, Jodie. I'm Ava. I'm your nurse while you're in recovery. You've had surgery on your hand. How's the pain?"

Strange how her hand could hurt so much yet feel so numb at the same time.

"It's okay." Her words slurred and she closed her eyes again. Memories were coming back. The agony. Being transferred to Walla Walla Hospital in the early hours of the morning. The surgeon's warning that she might lose her fingers. That she might never regain proper use of her hand.

She forced her eyes open again, desperate to ask the nurse about her fingers. She looked down, but her bandaged hand was a blur of white.

The nurse fiddled with the drip then walked away before Jodie could find her voice.

Thoughts swirled around, making her dizzy. She groaned. Why couldn't she think clearly?

Lord? I need your help.

Her mind began to clear, but she almost wished it didn't. She'd ruined Josh and Hallie's special night. Worse, she'd hurt Brandon. Badly. She'd thought keeping him at a distance was safest for both of them. She'd wrestled with feelings of attraction from the day she'd first met him. But no way was she going to love and lose someone else. He'd spent so much time with her family she'd had to tell herself he was a brother. Nothing more. And to do that, she'd needed to keep him in his place. Even if that meant calling him out on his faults, treating him as less spiritual, less deserving.

She held in a sob. What had she done? Last night, Brandon had needed her support, her understanding. Instead, she'd preached at him. And yes, she'd been condescending.

He'd opened up to her about his past for the first time ever, and she'd shoved it back in his face. Used it against him.

Then she'd tried to stop him driving off. Tried to grab his car door without warning. She was the one who was foolish around cars. What did she think would happen? That she'd be strong enough to stop him shutting the door? Strong enough to stop a moving car?

Now he'd be punishing himself for something that wasn't his fault. He wasn't to know she was stupid enough to try grabbing his door.

She looked down at her hand. What if she'd lost the use of her fingers? She loved typing. It was like making music on the keyboard as words flowed from her heart onto the page. Typing one-handed wasn't the same. What was a musician without full use of her instrument?

Another thought struck. There was no way she could move to New York this coming semester. She didn't need a doctor to know her hand would take months to heal, that she'd need regular PT and specialist appointments, that there were many things she wouldn't be able to handle on her own, one-handed. Which meant she'd lose her scholarship.

Tears welled up. She didn't bother trying to stop them as they dripped down her cheeks as the crushing weight of disappointment settled in her chest.

That scholarship was the only reason she could afford to go to NYU. No way was she going to take from what little her parents had.

She'd heard Hallie's mother once tell Mom that youngest children were always spoiled. Always the careless ones who expected everything handed to them on a platter.

That's why she'd struggled so hard to make sure she was independent, to not expect too much. She was going to reach the world with truth, using the media and her gift as a journalist to change lives … all on her own.

Now look at her. Broken. Useless. She deserved this. Deserved every broken bone in her body.

A machine beeped beside her and the nurse came back.

"Are you sure your pain levels are okay? Your blood pressure and pulse rate are too high for my liking."

Jodie drew in a deep breath. This wasn't physical pain. This was a deep, agonizing heartache that no painkillers could ever resolve.

CHAPTER TWELVE

Brandon called Josh first thing. He'd had a sleepless night, every accusation Jodie had ever thrown at him sinking deeper into his soul.

Josh answered straight away. "Brandon, I was about to call you. Jodie's doing well. She's been transferred to Walla Walla Hospital, and they think they've managed to save her fingers."

He should feel relieved. But he didn't. He needed to see her for himself.

Facing her again terrified him, but he remembered the quote from Nelson Mandela. *Courage isn't the absence of fear but the triumph over it.* He didn't deserve to connect his experience with anything to do with the noble Nelson Mandela, but he couldn't let Jodie go another day without knowing how sorry he was. If she tore him to shreds, he deserved it.

He drove carefully to Walla Walla, sticking to the speed limit for the first time in his life, flinching at every car he passed. Jodie was right. His car was a weapon. He was the handler. He was capable of seriously injuring someone. The responsibility weighed him down.

How could he have been proud of the way he ignored road

rules? Showed off the power of his vehicle and his ability to handle it? Used his speed to validate his own worth?

His heart was pounding by the time he arrived at the hospital. The large building towered before him, and once more he wanted to be sick. But this wasn't about him. He needed to pull himself together, go in there, and see the damage he'd caused.

"I'm looking for Jodie Ladan," he said to the receptionist.

She typed something into her computer, then gave him directions to the orthopedic ward. Some kind of alarm sounded and he winced as he continued down the hallway. He hated the sounds and smells of hospitals.

He could hear voices as he turned the corner into her room. He slowed. Her parents sat by her bed and there she lay, her hand bandaged, eyes closed. She was so pale.

"Brandon." Pastor Theo stood and to Brandon's surprise, pulled him into a fierce hug. "She's still very sleepy, but the plastic and orthopedic surgeons did a brilliant job. They think they've saved her fingers. She's a bit sleepy now—the pain meds do that."

"How long …?"

"Until we know for sure?" Pastor Theo looked hesitant.

"It went through the muscle, didn't it." He knew it had. "What about the nerves and tendons?"

"They were impacted but may also heal in time. We just have to wait and see."

Brandon should be relieved there was the chance she would heal, but his heart was still heavy. He studied her as she lay there, blonde hair fanned out around her on the pillow, eyes closed. Never had he so badly wanted her to look at him, to see those blue eyes, bright and alive, turned in his direction.

"Have a seat." Jodie's mother, Lil, stood. "I'm going to go and get something to eat." She looked at Theo. "You want anything?"

"A cup of coffee and a sandwich would be great."

Brandon watched Lil go. He should be offering to pay for their lunch. He swallowed hard and looked back at Theo.

"I'll pay for this."

"No you won't." Theo's words were strong, but his expression was gentle. "You have your mother's medical bills to take care of."

"She has insurance."

"So do we."

"It won't cover everything, and this was my fault."

Theo put an arm on Brandon's shoulder, giving him much needed comfort. "Not according to Jodie. She said you had no way of knowing she'd grab your door and try to stop you leaving."

Brandon bit his lip. Pastor Ladan was showing him a lot of grace when his daughter lay there with her hand broken, her plans for her future hanging in the balance.

"Will she still be able to go to New York?"

Pastor Theo hesitated and it answered his question. Guilt pressed down. "What did they say?"

"They can't hold her place or the scholarship. And she can't go this semester because she'll need help with everyday tasks at first. She'll also need checkups and ongoing therapy."

Brandon knew how hard it was to work one-handed. He'd broken his arm playing basketball when he was ten. He'd never realised how much he used his left hand for everyday tasks. "Can I talk to her?"

"Of course." Theo moved his chair to the side to allow Brandon past.

Brandon studied the monitors and tubes attached to her, then touched her arm. "Jodie?"

Her eyes opened but she looked dazed.

"It's me. Brandon."

A slow, beautiful smile filled her face, bringing an unexpected lump to his throat. Why was she looking at him like that? "You came," she murmured.

"Yes, I came to say I'm sorry. I'm so, so sorry." His voice caught and she frowned.

"No," she mumbled. "No." Tears welled in her eyes, and she turned her face away.

He moved to touch her, to explain again that he was in agony for what he'd done. "Jodie?" he whispered.

She shook her head. His heart hurt. She'd never forgive him. He didn't blame her.

"Everything okay in here?" A nurse marched in and fiddled with the machine by Jodie's bed. She looked down at Jodie. "How's the pain?"

Jodie gave the slightest shake of her head.

"You've got none?" the nurse asked, her tone officious. "On a scale of one to ten, where is your pain?"

Jodie bit her lip, and Brandon realized what the problem was. She didn't want to admit her pain in front of him. That was so like Jodie. He stepped away from the bed.

"I'll go," he whispered to Theo.

Theo nodded while Brandon slipped out the door and made his way down the hall. He'd wanted to tell that impatient nurse to have a bit of understanding, but who was he to tell someone to treat Jodie better? His terrible treatment of her was the reason she was there.

———

Bruce gave Brandon a wave as he came into the workshop Monday morning. "I heard about your friend. How is she?"

That was Trinity Lakes for you. Everyone knew everything.

"I think she's going to be okay." No thanks to him, but he couldn't bring himself to admit that to Bruce. Even if Jodie had grabbed his door, he shouldn't have driven off so fast.

"Good to hear." Bruce rubbed his hands down his overalls. "Susannah Gilbertson called a few minutes ago. Reckons you left the smell of smoke in her car. Wants a discount on her bill."

Brandon rolled his eyes. "I don't smoke." His mother did, but he never had.

"I know." Bruce shook his head. "That woman is a menace. She needs to be stopped."

Brandon bit his lip. He knew information that could ruin her and her ex-husband's reputation, but it would also affect Susannah's daughters—his cousins, Becky and Hannah. They didn't deserve to suffer because their mother had a lack of ethics.

Brandon's phone rang. He ignored it.

"I'll finish up on the Cohen's truck," he said. Jasper had hardware deliveries to make, so the sooner he fixed his work vehicle, the better.

His phone rang again. He let it ring as he picked up the key fob for the vehicle with "Cohen's Hardware" splashed down the side.

His phone stopped and immediately the work phone rang. Something settled deep in his gut. A feeling. A knowing that something was terribly wrong.

He watched as Bruce picked it up. Watched Bruce's smile turn down, his forehead crease. His gaze flicked Brandon's way.

And he knew.

"Phone for you, Brandon," he said. "It's your father."

Brandon took the cordless phone from Bruce's hand. "Dad?"

"Your mother's nurse called me, son. She's lost consciousness. She doesn't have long. I'm coming to get you now and take you home."

He'd known it was coming. Thought he'd prepared himself. But the way his hands trembled and something inside him died told him nothing could ever have prepared him for this day. He hadn't realized how much he had hoped, dreamed, even believed his mother would get better.

Bruce patted him on the shoulder. "Don't even think about work, you hear? You go home and look after your mother."

His father arrived minutes later. On weighted legs, Brandon climbed into his truck. Dad didn't speak. His green eyes said it all. He felt Brandon's pain, felt his own pain. Brandon's mother had betrayed him many years ago and kept Brandon's existence a secret, but Dad still cared. He could see it in his eyes.

"You want me to come in?" Dad asked when they arrived outside the house.

Brandon nodded, unable to speak. Pastor Ladan had said he would come when this day came, but he was in the hospital with Jodie. There was no way Brandon was going to call him away from Jodie's bedside.

Mom's nurse stood and motioned Brandon in when he arrived at the door. A candle filled the dim room with a pleasant scent. It reminded Brandon of the smell of his grandparents' house, where he'd spent most of his growing up years. Quiet music played in the background, at odds with the heavy pounding of Brandon's heart.

His gaze went to his mother. She looked so peaceful. Her hands and feet had been swelling more these past few days. He'd kidded himself it was okay, that it wasn't a sign she was near the end.

"Mom?" He knelt beside the bed and took her hand. "Can you hear me?"

Her hand moved, closing loosely around his.

"I love you, Mom." His voice cracked. "And I'm going to see you again one day."

Mom drew in a raspy breath. Her eyes opened. She smiled, her eyes fixed on some faraway place. "I see him," she whispered. "I see him."

"Who?" Brandon spun his head around to look. The nurse

was waiting outside the door. His father was over by the window. Who was Mom smiling at?

She lifted her arms ever so slightly. "Jesus."

The word was spoken softly, with reverence. For a moment Brandon wondered if he'd misheard, but one glance at Dad showed he hadn't. Dad's face was filled with wonder.

"He loves me." She closed her eyes.

Brandon stared at his mother. The coarse, mocking woman of his childhood had been replaced with this gentle, loving woman. He'd seen the change over the past six months since her diagnosis, since she'd desperately searched for hope, for reason to believe in life after death. After Pastor Ladan introduced her to Jesus, Brandon had seen the softening, the gentling, but he'd never understood the depth of it until now.

"It's okay," the nurse said. "It's a common phenomenon when people are nearing the end. Sometimes they'll see loved ones who have passed on, sometimes an angel or another spiritual figure."

Loved ones. He and his mother had very few loved ones. Who would he see in his dying hours? A picture of Jodie came to mind and he pushed it away.

Jesus. He wanted to see Jesus. Like his mother.

His mind went back to the day he had come to believe in Jesus.

"Talk to her," the nurse encouraged.

Brandon swallowed hard. "Mom, do you remember the day I told you I'd become a Christian?"

She didn't move, but the peaceful smile remained, despite her rattly breaths.

"I didn't tell you the full story. There was a girl at school, Ariel. I'd had a crush on her for years, but when one of my friends told her, she said she couldn't consider me as a potential boyfriend because I wasn't a Christian. I was furious because I thought she thought she was better than me. I did everything I could to bring her down. I mocked her, belittled her, tried to find arguments against her faith to prove she was giving up her life for a fantasy." His smile turned rueful. "Yeah, I know, true love, right? But she never retaliated."

He drew in a deep breath. "The summer before we moved here, she died. Had an anaphylactic reaction. Her best friend, Paige, came up to me one day at school and gave me something. It was a Bible. She said Ariel's family wanted me to have it and that they had photocopied some pages of Ariel's journal for me."

Brandon closed his eyes as he remembered that day. His hands had shaken as he'd shoved the Bible and the letter in his backpack. He knew what would be in there. Ariel would have written about how miserable he'd made her life. How he deserved to burn in hell for all he'd done. Did her family think that giving him the Bible would drive the guilt he deserved deeper into his heart?

He'd shoved the Bible in his bottom drawer. He would have thrown it out except that felt irreverent. It took him two troubled days and two sleepless nights before he finally opened the sealed envelope with the journal pages.

What he read there changed his life.

Lord, I know Brandon's hurting. Please show him your love and forgiveness. You know how hard it's been for me, not responding to his feelings for me. To wait on your timing. He keeps up this protective barrier, and only You can break it down. Protect my heart, Lord. Keep me strong. And save Brandon's soul.

Entry after entry was filled with prayers for him. She'd spent the final months of her life praying for him. That he would know Jesus.

Her final entry changed something deep in his soul.

Lord, when I arrive in heaven, please let Brandon Taylor be there too.

She'd entered eternity before him. As he'd read her words,

he saw a vision of her face. She was glowing with beauty, in the arms of God.

He'd begun reading the Bible, but not told anyone. And one night, by himself in his room, he'd given his life to Jesus. It wasn't until he moved here to Trinity Lakes that he'd begun going to church and found a spiritual family in the Ladans.

"Mom," Brandon said softly, "When you get to heaven, please give Ariel a hug and thank her for all her prayers for me. Tell her I'll see her there someday."

Brandon let his head fall onto the bed, exhausted. He felt a hand on his shoulder. Dad. He'd forgotten he was here. He looked up to see his father's eyes glistening.

"You did good, son," he whispered. Then he nodded toward Mom. "Mind if I talk to her?"

"Not at all." Brandon moved aside but continued holding his mother's hand.

"Mariah? It's Luke." His Dad's throat bobbed. "I have so many regrets. I should have been a better partner. I should have chased after you when you left. I'm not a fighter, but when it came to you, I should have been. We both made mistakes, but I want you to know, everything will be okay. I will be there for Brandon every step of the way. I will fight for him. You can count on me."

Mom didn't show that she'd heard, but Dad's face relaxed and Brandon knew he'd needed to get the words off his chest.

He listened to Mom's breathing. Every now and then her breaths would stop for a few minutes, then another would come.

"It's okay," the nurse reassured them. "She's not in pain."

Brandon wanted to thank the nurse, but the words stuck in his throat. She'd been so compassionate and gentle. He didn't know what they'd have done without her this past month.

"It won't be long now," she said.

The nurse knew the medical signs, but Brandon also knew it

was time. It was as though a holy presence had filled the room. Peace like he'd never known flowed over him, and warmth filled his soul like it had when he'd first told Jesus he believed in Him. He knew it wasn't always like this. The final moments before death weren't always so beautiful, but this was God's gift to him. A taste of the eternity Mom was now entering. God knew he didn't deserve it. God knew Mom didn't either. But this was grace.

Mom exhaled and then lay still. So still.

"She's gone."

Brandon didn't know how much time had passed, but the nurse's words didn't bring horror the way he'd thought they would. He felt the wetness on his cheeks, the tears as they dripped off his chin, but there wasn't the raw agony he'd expected. Because God was here.

"I love you, Mom," he said, then wrapped his arms around her one final time.

Oh God, I know you're here. Jesus, I feel you. Thank you.

The music in the background washed over him and the words of Chris Tomlin's *I Will Rise* filled his soul. Jesus had overcome. Mom was safe in His arms. Loved. Complete. Brandon lifted his arms, releasing her into the arms of Jesus.

Jesus had called Mom's name, and she was home.

CHAPTER THIRTEEN

Jodie wanted to go home. Her night nurse had been nicer than yesterday's, but the hospital sounds kept her awake. The beeping of machines drilled into her skull and she couldn't cover both ears with her right hand the way it was. She attempted to straighten her pillowslip but gave up in frustration. It was impossible. She'd tried texting Josh but it was so slow one-handed. And even turning on the phone was difficult. She'd managed to use her elbow to hold her phone steady still while turning it on with her other hand. And when she'd held a full bottle of water between her knees to open the lid, water had gushed like a fountain out the top, wetting her jeans. And changing out of the wet jeans … she'd had to ask the nurse for help. It was frustrating and humiliating. It didn't help that it was her dominant hand out of action.

She attempted a smile as Mom came into the room. "Good morning. Where's Dad?"

Mom leaned over the bed and gave her a hug, then sat down in the chair beside her. "Oh, sweetheart, he had to go home. Josh called late last night. Mariah Taylor went to be with Jesus yesterday."

"What?" Jodie gasped. Poor Brandon. She couldn't breathe. Couldn't think.

"It happened very quickly. She went peacefully. Brandon was by her side."

Jodie bit her lip but couldn't stop the tears that built up then poured down her cheeks. Dad had arranged for a healing evangelist to come to their church a few weeks back. He'd prayed for Mariah, and Jodie had believed she would be healed. Or maybe she'd wanted it so badly she'd convinced herself it would happen.

"Oh, Brandon."

"I know." Mom's eyes glistened. "Dad's with him now. He traveled home late last night. He said Brandon's holding up well, considering."

Everything within Jodie wanted to be there too. "I need to go home."

"We'll see what the doctor says."

Mom didn't understand how urgent it was. Jodie needed to ask Brandon's forgiveness. To tell him that what happened wasn't his fault. She stared down at her hand and wept tears of frustration.

"God's got him, Jodie. He'll be all right."

Jodie lay back against her pillows. Mom was right. It was her pride thinking she had to be the one to speak to Brandon, to comfort him. It was the same pride that had caused her to challenge him all these years, to try to change him and fix him. And that's how she'd ended up here in the hospital. She needed to trust God with Brandon.

Oh God, I wish I could see him. Please, please hold him tight today.

———

THE DOCTOR finally came in at midday and agreed to discharge Jodie.

"I'm happy with how you're doing, but we won't know if you'll regain full use of your hand for several months. Maybe even a year. In the meantime, you need to see a local physical therapist regularly and make sure you don't overuse your hand. I've heard Adam Lancaster is in Trinity Lakes. He comes highly recommended."

Mom nodded. "We know him from church."

"Great. I'll write up a referral." The surgeon patted Jodie's head as though she were a little girl. "You take care of yourself, you hear?"

Jodie nodded, but her mind was racing in all directions. Everything in her life had changed so quickly. Had God merely delayed her dreams, or was he redirecting? She trusted God. She really did. But it didn't take away the deep disappointment that His plans were not her plans.

She watched as Mom pottered around, packing her things. Josh and Hallie had come to visit yesterday afternoon and had brought some items from home. She been glad to get out of the hospital gown and into her own clothes ... with Mom's help. She grimaced. Nothing like needing your mother's help for every little thing. It was like being a toddler again.

———

BRANDON SAT in the Ladan's living room with Josh and Theo as they went over funeral details. He was so grateful for them. Grateful for the way Josh had dropped everything to be there for him. It bothered him that Theo had left Jodie in the hospital to be here, but it warmed his heart too. This family cared for him like their own.

"I'd like the song, *I will rise* by Chris Tomlin," Brandon said. He swallowed down the lump in his throat. Mom had taken her last breath while it was playing.

Theo wrote it down. "What about Bible passages? Any thoughts?"

Brandon rubbed the back of his neck. "Something about grace."

Theo smiled. "That gives me lots of options."

"And about us being new creations."

"That verse in Corinthians. 2 Corinthians 5:17." Theo nodded and wrote that down, too.

The front door opened and Brandon looked up. Jodie. He blinked, unable to think for a moment. His gaze flew to her hand. A short cast covered the back of her arm and hand, and her fingers were still heavily bandaged.

She blinked rapidly and bit her trembling lip. Tears filled her eyes as she stood looking at him. She shook her head and opened her mouth to speak but no words came.

He gave her a half-smile, his heart pounding against his chest. "Welcome home."

He was vaguely aware that the rest of the family had disappeared.

She shook her head and her chin quivered. "Brandon, I'm so, so sorry." Her voice broke.

"It's okay." How could he explain to her the grace of God and how beautiful God had made his mother's passing?

"No. No it's not. Your mother was dying and I … you had enough to deal with, and I was so graceless. So … proud. You're right. I can be a condescending little know-it-all and I'm so, so sorry."

She was still so pale. She looked like she might fall at any minute. He jumped up, came to her side. Her eyes widened when he put his arm around her, but she allowed him to guide her to the couch. Her beautiful blue eyes glistened, but her gaze never left him.

He sat down and turned sideways to face her.

"Jodie, you were right. About everything you said. About my

driving. About me mocking and belittling people. No wonder you can't trust me. Look how I treated my own father before I knew who he was."

Dismay filled her features. She cleared her throat. "You have changed. You really have. I have no right to hold the past against you. And even if anything I said was right, it wasn't helpful. It wasn't kind."

"Isn't speaking the truth more important than being kind?"

"No." She shook her head. "No, it's not. Those things I said shouldn't have come from me. Not the way they did. God convicts and forgives. It's the enemy who condemns."

Brandon looked down and rubbed the back of his neck. He had to admit he'd felt condemned.

"I don't want to be an instrument of the enemy," she whispered. She touched his hand and warmth spread all the way up his arm to his heart. "I want to be your friend."

He tried to smile but it came out lopsided. His chin trembled. "I could do with friends right now."

"I know. I could too. Brandon, I want to have the courage to stop shutting you out. To stop being so selfish and self-protective."

He looked at her left hand resting on his arm. She followed his gaze then jerked it back to her side. He held in his smile. She didn't need to worry. He knew she wasn't flirting.

Before he could think it through, he pulled her hand back and held it in his. It felt small in his large, work-roughened one. He threaded their fingers together. "Friends," he said softly.

She blushed furiously and stared at their hands now resting together on his knee but she didn't try to pull away.

"Real friends," she said, tears pooling in her blue eyes. "I want to be here for you, to listen—really listen—because I've realized you can't listen when you've got something to prove. No more trying to prove myself, no walls, no protecting myself against pain or loss."

He couldn't speak. Couldn't comprehend the magnitude of this gift she was offering him. He looked away, fighting the burn in his eyes.

She cleared her throat. "So if there's anything I can do to help with your mom's funeral …" She lifted her injured hand. "As long as it's something I can do one-handed."

He smiled, though the words "mom" and "funeral" in the same sentence still jarred him. "Do you think you could sort through old photos and pick some nice ones of Mom for me?"

"I can do that." She was so close, her eyes gazing into his full of sincerity and compassion. "But I might be a bit slow."

He chuckled. "What's new?"

She pulled her hand from his and playfully swatted him. He missed the warmth of her touch, but it was safer to have space between them. He stood and looked around for the rest of the family.

"Mom. Dad," Jodie hollered, and Brandon grinned. This was the Jodie he knew and … well, knew.

The family appeared again and gathered around him.

"I'm wrecked," Jodie said. "I'm going to take some painkillers and lie down for a bit." She stood. "But I can help look through photos later this afternoon."

"I'll bring her over to your place when she wakes up," Josh said. "I'll help, too."

His place. Brandon swallowed. It was just his place now. "Thanks. Both of you. I appreciate it."

Jodie made her way upstairs to her room, her steps slower than usual. Brandon tried not to watch her. Her golden ponytail swung from side to side as she walked and her jeans fitted her to perfection. She was beautiful. Like Ariel. Deep down, he knew that was part of the reason he'd not allowed himself to fall for Jodie over the years. Ariel had died so he could come to know Jesus. If Jodie … He didn't even know how to finish the thought. It didn't make sense and yet it was there, swimming around somewhere in the back of his brain, taunting him, challenging him.

"Would you like help writing the eulogy?" Theo's question brought him back to the present.

"That would be great. I don't even know where to start."

CHAPTER FOURTEEN

Jodie sifted through photos from Mariah Taylor's memory box one at a time. It was slow work with only one hand, but Brandon didn't seem to mind. He and Josh sorted through digital photos on the computer.

She picked up a photo that lay face down and turned it over. Brandon? But who was the young woman he was gazing at with such love? A twinge of dismay filled her until truth dawned. This was an old photo. The young man wasn't Brandon, it was Luke McAffrey—the Junk Man, Brandon's father. And the woman he had his arm around was Brandon's mother.

"Wow," she muttered. "Brandon, look at this." Brandon swiveled around on the office chair and reached to take it.

His eyes widened. "He looks like me."

"Doesn't he? I don't know how no one in town worked out who you are."

He chuckled softly. "That long scraggly beard Dad used to have might have something to do with it."

"True."

He handed the photo back, and Jodie set it aside. Even if the photo of Luke and Mariah wasn't used at the funeral, it was a picture worth having around to remind Brandon of a time his parents had loved one another.

She turned over more photos, smiling at the baby pictures of Brandon. He was a cute baby. Not surprising. He was still cute. She looked at each picture that showed his growing up years. His mom obviously adored him. There weren't many photos of them together, but Jodie knew it was because his mother was usually behind the camera.

"Aw ..." The photo of Brandon's first day of school was precious. Someone else had obviously taken the photo because he stood beside his mom with a huge smile on his face, his school backpack looking oversized on his small frame.

Brandon swiveled in the chair again. "What is it?"

She handed him the photo. "How cute were you?"

To her surprise, he didn't make some smart comeback. He actually blushed and handed it back to her.

"We have to use this one," she said. "Maybe on the back of the order of service?"

Brandon shrugged as he spun back to the computer screen. "Okay."

He was kind of adorable when he was embarrassed. She didn't think she'd ever seen him blush before.

Jodie set aside suitable photos for Brandon to look through, including a professional studio portrait of his mother as a young woman.

"There might be stuff in there that we can use too," Brandon said, pointing to a larger box on the table. "It's from before we moved here."

Jodie opened it and pulled out a photo of Brandon at around the age of six or seven standing beside a race car, his grandfather by his side. The pride and joy in his young face was undeniable. She fought back emotion. For so long, she'd attacked something he loved. Something precious to him.

She looked up to where Josh continued to look through

photos while Brandon looked down at his phone, his brow furrowed.

He looked up and caught her gaze. "I'm looking for that verse about new creations," he said. "Your dad said it was 5 Corinthians or something."

Josh chuckled. "Maybe 2 Corinthians?"

Brandon's grin was sheepish. "Yeah, maybe."

Jodie looked back down. The pull to hug him, to protect him, was strong.

She lifted the next item from the box. It was an old, well-used Bible, but it looked feminine. Surprised, she flipped through it. Some parts were highlighted in pink. There were notes in some of the margins. She flipped back to the front of the Bible. Who did it belong to?

Ariel Pereira.

The name was written in a beautiful calligraphy with sweeping letters. And there, in the front, was a funeral order of service.

In loving memory of Ariel.

A picture of a beautiful girl smiled up at her, with a birth and death date underneath. Jodie did a quick calculation. This girl, Ariel, was born twenty-four years ago. She died when she was about sixteen. She must have been the same age as Brandon.

She opened the funeral sheet. It was beautifully done.

"Brandon," she said tentatively. "I found this Bible, and this was in here. It might give you some ideas."

Brandon turned around and took the order of service from her hand. Then he went pale. His hand trembled as he studied the image of the beautiful girl.

Who was she? Brandon's girlfriend? Was she the reason he avoided committing to any relationship? Was he still in love with Ariel Pereira? The girl whose Bible he'd kept?

———

IT HAD BEEN YEARS, but Brandon would recognize Ariel's picture anywhere. His heart pounded.

"I'm sorry," Jodie said, her big blue eyes filled with compassion. "I should've been more sensitive." She looked near to tears.

"It's okay." He stood. He itched to open the order of service, but not in front of Josh and Jodie. Even when he'd read Ariel's journal entries and her Bible all those years ago, he hadn't been able to open the order of service. It made it all too final. Too real.

"I'm going to sit outside for a while." He took the sheet and went out onto the back porch step, into the warm spring air. It was May, the first month of his life he'd lived without his mother. Mom's cigarette butts littered the ground, and unexpected sorrow stabbed his heart.

"Oh, Mom, if only you'd been able to quit smoking." So many if onlys. His hands shook as he opened the order of service.

He glanced through lyrics of songs he didn't know. Paige Merrin was listed to speak after the eulogy. Ariel's best friend. His heart pained as he remembered the way he'd picked on Paige. She was a smart girl, also a Christian. He'd thought he was funny but he'd also been cruel.

His eyes moved to the next page.

Psalm One—Ariel's life Psalm.

He read the Psalm, and his throat closed up. Ariel had been a tree planted by rivers of water. The River of Life. She had produced much fruit. She had stood firm through all his taunts, the verbal arrows he'd thrown her way.

He read verse one again.

Blessed is the one who does not walk in step with the wicked or stand in the way that sinners take or sit in the company of mockers,

His heart skipped a beat. He and his mother had sat in the company of mockers their whole lives. They *were* the mockers.

Oh, Lord. His heart filled with sorrow at all the seemingly harmless comments he'd made about people. He'd ridiculed his own father for years. True, Mom had encouraged him, put the ideas in his head. But …

I have not been a tree planted by the rivers of life. He lifted his chin. "Until now."

Things were going to change. With God's help, he would be different. He would speak only words of life.

Jodie came out to sit beside him. He still held the funeral service sheet in his hand. He passed it over to her.

"A girl in my class at school," he said. "She's the reason I became a Christian."

Jodie bit her lip, fumbling to open the service sheet one-handed. He reached over and opened it for her. He pointed to the third page. "Her life Psalm."

Jodie read it. She didn't speak.

Brandon swallowed hard. "I want to speak words of life. I don't want to sit in the seat of mockers. I don't want to be one of the wicked."

"You are God's child," Jodie reminded him quietly. "You are a new creation, being renewed day by day."

Brandon chuckled and it came out hollow. "I haven't helped with the process though."

"Neither have I."

His eyes locked with hers. Understanding and awareness sparked between them.

"I looked up some verses on my phone while I was in the hospital," Jodie said. "I couldn't sleep." She stood to pull her phone out of her back pocket but couldn't manage while holding the order of service as well. She let out a frustrated sigh as she fumbled one-handed.

Brandon bit back his smile as he watched. She was so independent "Want some help?"

She blushed furiously, then her shoulders dropped in defeat.

"Or maybe you could hold this for me." She held out the order of service.

He grinned. "I could. Not as enjoyable."

Her eyes widened in shock, and he immediately regretted his words. "Sorry. Not appropriate."

She bit her lip and it was clear she was trying not to smile. "Can you look up 2 Timothy 4:12 on your phone for me?"

Brandon found it and read it out. "Don't let anyone look down on you because you are young, but set an example for the believers in speech, in conduct, in love, in faith and in purity."

Jodie blinked hard. "May God help me speak the truth in love. I want to speak only truth, life, and love."

He nodded. "Me too."

He turned the funeral sheet over again and studied Ariel's picture.

"She's pretty." Jodie said. "How did she die?"

The sympathy in her tone almost undid him. "Anaphylactic shock. She didn't know she was allergic to seafood. After she died, her family gave me her Bible. She'd written in her journal about me. She prayed that I'd become a Christian."

"And you did." Jodie's eyes turned soft. "That must be such a joy for her family to know."

He cleared his throat. "Actually, they don't know."

"What? You have to tell them. It would bring them such joy."

"Wouldn't it be hard to know their daughter died so I could become a Christian?"

"Brandon, don't think that way. God planned every one of Ariel's days before she was born. Taking her death on yourself is giving the enemy way too much credit. God's plans are beyond all we can ever imagine."

Was she right? Should he tell Ariel's family?

Jodie let out a big sigh. "Life is so fragile. We never know how long we've got, do we?"

He shook his head. No. And he was tired of wasting his life

on empty, meaningless, and even hurtful words. He would speak truth in love. He would speak life. If that included him going to see Ariel's family, he would do it.

CHAPTER FIFTEEN

Jodie watched Brandon as he stood by his mother's graveside a week after her death. He looked so different from the laid-back Brandon she was used to. Gone was the amused smile, the knowing look, the grease-covered work clothes. Today he was dressed in a black suit, head bowed, dark hair hanging over his forehead. He looked older, as though the loss of his mother had aged him several years. The grief etched on his face hurt her heart. She wanted to wrap her arms around him, hold him tight, but she kept her distance and prayed for him instead.

He was surrounded by people today. The church had showered him with love and support. His father stood on one side and his cousin, Becky, stood on the other. Jodie wondered if Becky knew the part her father had played in bringing Brandon's father down years ago.

Her mind went back to Brandon's request to write an article that would help prevent his father's eviction. Could Becky help? Would she be willing to speak against her own parents? She put the thought aside. A funeral was not the right place for investigation. She'd have plenty of time in the upcoming months while she waited for her hand to heal. How she'd type up the reports was another story. It would be frustratingly slow typing one-handed. Perhaps she should get Brandon to put the voice-to-text app he'd set up for Josh on her laptop as well.

She glanced around her and froze. Becky's father, Wayne Gilbertson, was here. He stood at the back of the group of mourners beside Mariah's nurse, almost as though he didn't want to be seen. She saw him wipe away a tear. The man genuinely cared! Her mind began to put the pieces together. Brandon had said someone paid for his mother's full-time nurse, but his mother wouldn't say who. Would Wayne have done that? He was Mariah's cousin, after all. Maybe the man had a bigger heart than she'd realized. Once again, she'd judged too quickly.

Dad's voice drew her mind back. He spoke about Mariah Taylor's trust in Jesus and Jodie forced herself to focus. Mariah's conversion had been a miracle. Her diagnosis of cancer had made her seriously think about life, death, and life after death. Jodie pictured Mariah in heaven with Jesus, and her heart lifted.

It was a sad day, but in death there was life. Eternal life.

———

BRANDON TOLERATED the funeral repast as best he could. Mom didn't even like half these people. Strange who came out of the woodwork when someone died. He was grateful for the church ladies who provided the refreshments in the church hall—really —but he wasn't in the mood for small talk.

"I'm sorry for your loss, Brandon." Becky Gilbertson stood in front of him, her compassion stinging his eyes.

"Thank you. And thank you for coming."

She nodded. "Hannah would've come, but..."

"I understand." And he did. Susannah would be upset enough

that Becky was here. If her other daughter had come, she would feel completely betrayed.

"Let me know if there's anything I can do."

He knew Becky meant it. Everyone did. But what was there to do? Mom was in heaven and it was so final. A good kind of final. He wouldn't wish her back here on earth to suffer again, but he missed her.

"If you ever need company, ever need family around, I'm here," Becky said.

Brandon swallowed hard. "That means a lot. Really."

She smiled, then gave him a hug. "You're like a brother to me. You're family."

Jodie had said the same thing. Jodie. He glanced around. Where was she? He'd heard Rhonda Ingalls ask what had happened to her hand and she'd graciously said she'd jammed it in a car door. Nothing about him.

Was it rude to escape his own mother's funeral? He wanted to see Jodie. He slipped out the door.

"Brandon. You okay?"

He stopped and turned. Jodie sat on the steps at the side of the church. Her plastered hand rested on her knees. Her blue eyes met his, beautiful, filled with compassion.

With a weary smile he sank down beside her. "Doing well, considering. You?"

She shrugged. "It's all very intense, isn't it?"

"Yeah."

She let out a huge sigh, a sigh he knew was for him, for his pain. Then she rested her head on his shoulder. Wisps of her soft, golden blonde hair tickled his neck and something in his heart melted. The loneliness and turmoil evaporated. Jodie understood him. She really understood him. And the fact she shared his sorrow and seemed to get him on a soul-deep level somehow lessened the pain. He hadn't realized how much he craved connection with her.

They sat there together in silence, just breathing, being. Jodie was holding the space his mother had always held for him and so much more. He knew then that God would never leave him alone. He would provide. Whatever he needed, whomever he needed, God would provide. Peace washed over his heart and settled deep in his soul.

CHAPTER SIXTEEN

Jodie huffed out a sigh as she fumbled with Dad's shirt then watched it fall to the grass. Life with one hand was hard. She felt useless.

"What's up with you?"

She started at the sound of Brandon's voice. He came across the back yard toward her.

"How'd you get here?"

He nodded toward the side gate. "It was open." He stopped in front of her. "What's wrong?"

"Nothing." Except her hand hurt. And she was frustrated. And sad.

"Nothing." Brandon scowled, mimicking her, then chuckled.

A reluctant smile stretched her mouth. "Okay, I'm just … well, I wanted to hang the laundry for Mom, but …" She indicated the shirt on the ground.

He picked it up and pegged it on the line. "And?"

How did he read her so well? "And I guess I'm feeling a bit sad and lost. It's quiet at home. I never thought I'd say it, but I miss Josh now he and Hallie are … "

"In love." He studied her for a moment. "You're jealous?"

"He's my brother."

Brandon took another shirt from the basket and bent to take some clothespins from the bucket. "I mean of their relationship. You're no longer the most important girl in your brother's world, and you're no longer Hallie's best friend. You've lost two in one."

With a sigh, Jodie sat down on the garden wall, while Brandon continued hanging the clothes.

"I was never the most important girl in Josh's world. That was Esther."

"Ah. The elusive sister." Brandon pegged a sock on the line. "Still no contact with her?"

"Mom talked with her briefly the other night. But this isn't just about me. You've lost your Mom. And you've also lost your best friend to Hallie."

To her surprise, he turned and smiled until his eyes crinkled in the corners.

"What?"

"I think it's all turned out very nicely."

"How can you say that?"

"Don't be like that." Brandon laughed and came over to touch the wrinkle in her forehead. "You'll scare someone."

Confusion washed over her. He was acting familiar, almost as though there was something between them.

He continued gazing at her with that tender, amused look. "Think about it. Mom is no longer in pain. She's living a life we could never dream of in heaven with Jesus. And Josh? He'll always be my friend, but now I have the time to get to know you." He came and pulled himself up onto the wall beside her. "Josh's been a great friend. He's good for a laugh, for company, for good times. But it's you God brought along to comfort me in my grief."

"Josh has done that too."

"Yes, but you ..." Brandon's voice turned deep and soft.

"Well, you were exactly who I needed. You understand loss. And you've helped me turn to God in my pain rather than away. You've got no idea how much I thank God for you."

He jumped off the wall and went back to pegging clothes. Jodie watched him, not knowing what to think. Brandon had just made it clear she held a special place in his heart. She didn't quite know what to do with that.

He finished hanging the laundry and turned back to her.

"I'll never understand why you hang your clothes out on the line. It's so much easier to dump them in the dryer."

Jodie smiled. "It's Mom's Australian childhood coming out. It was hot and dry where she lived in Queensland. Some days, she could hang the laundry at four in the afternoon and bring it in an hour later."

Brandon shuddered. "Give me the cool of the lakes and mountains any day. There's no place like Trinity Lakes."

BRANDON FELT a strong connection with Jodie as they sat together on the garden wall. The awful grief of the last few days had dissipated, but they were both feeling lost.

"Why aren't you at work?" she asked.

He dropped his mouth open in mock offense and pointed to her clothesline. "I just did work."

"You know what I mean." She smiled.

He shrugged and huffed out a sigh. "Bruce said I have to take another couple of weeks off—he's insisting I use up some of my accrued vacation leave. He's worried I work too much and says I need to take the time to grieve Mom properly. He doesn't understand that I need to have something to do."

"So what are you going to do?" Jodie picked up the laundry basket in one hand. She nodded toward the house, clearly expecting him to follow her inside.

"I don't know." It was the truth. He opened the back door for her. Two weeks was a long time to be alone with his thoughts, alone in the big house that was now his.

"You could visit Ariel's parents," Jodie dumped the basket in the laundry room and turned back to look at him.

"I could." He followed her into the living room. He looked around the familiar room and settled into one of the comfortable couches.

In the past he would have been sitting here with Josh, not Jodie.

The half-grown ginger kitten Josh had given Hallie was curled up on the floor.

He looked across at Jodie. "If I were to contact them …" Her eyes softened, giving him courage. "Would you be willing to help me?"

She smiled. "Of course. What do you want to do? Look online?"

"I don't know." Brandon clicked his tongue. "Doesn't that feel a bit stalkerish? Maybe we can ask Sheriff Thompson."

"Who will probably tell us to look online." Jodie's eyes twinkled at him.

"If he says that, then we will." He rubbed his hands down his jeans. "Would you be willing to come with me to ask him?"

Jodie's face fell. "I'd love to but I have a physical therapy appointment in about ten minutes. I'm just waiting for Mom to get home to take me. She's volunteering at the museum this morning."

Brandon had heard the museum was to be reopened on the twenty-fifth of May. Local history lover Ellie Reilly was supervising the project and doing a good job, from what he'd heard. He'd also heard they needed volunteers, but he hadn't had time. Until now.

"We should help." He grinned at Jodie. "I'm sure there's things you can do one-handed."

Jodie bit her lip. "I don't know …"

"Come on. You need to get out and about in this town. You need to make new friends. Goodbyes are hard, but the friends we make at the hellos make it all worth it."

Would she take offense? One side of her mouth lifted. "Yeah, I know. I need to stop being so insulated."

"Exactly. You need to learn to live. To really live."

She grinned. "And you're the one who can show me how to do that?"

He blinked exaggeratedly. "Well, not to boast or anything, but I'm pretty good at it."

She laughed, then looked down at her watch, forehead creasing. "Mom's late."

"Call her. Tell her I'm taking you to your appointment."

"What?"

He took out his phone. "I'll text her. Come on, let's go. Can't be late for your PT."

"You sure?"

"Absolutely." He typed furiously on his phone then showed it to her. "I've already sent the text." He shot her a mischievous smile. "I'll do this for you, then you can come to the sheriff's office with me. Grab your things. Let's go."

"Bossy, bossy," she said, but she was smiling as she collected her purse.

Brandon opened his truck door for her, then helped her with her seat belt. She bit her lip as he leaned over her to clip it into place. What would she do if he stopped on the way past to kiss her?

Stop it.

"Thank you," she whispered when he straightened the belt, not wanting to step away from her just yet.

He paused and his eyes locked with hers. "My pleasure."

And he meant it.

———

ADAM LANCASTER WAS WAITING for her when they arrived.

"Sorry I'm late," Jodie said. She was nervous. Her hand was still painful, and she had no idea what Adam would expect her to do, what agony PT would flare up again. Brandon's attentiveness had also set her on edge. She liked it. And that made it dangerous. Made him dangerous. Sure, she wanted to open her heart, but she didn't want to be reckless, to invite unnecessary hurt.

"No worries." Adam motioned them into the office at the front of his home. "Come in. Both of you."

Brandon shot her a questioning look and she smiled and dipped her head toward the office. "Come on. You don't get to sit out there, doing nothing. If I suffer, you have to suffer."

"That's what I like to hear. At least you understand the pain I'm about to inflict on you." Adam grinned.

She bit her lip. At least he was joking about it. That meant it wouldn't be too severe … didn't it?

Adam tapped a letter on his desk. "I received your referral. How's it feeling?"

"Still a bit tender. Much less pain than at first, though."

Adam nodded and reached for her hand. "Your surgeon has said I can take out the stitches if they're ready, or you can travel back to Walla Walla and he'll do it."

Jodie drew in a deep breath. Just the thought of stitches made her feel weak. "Have you done it before?"

"Many times, although I understand if you'd prefer the surgeon did it."

Fear warred with common sense. The surgeon would cost more. A trip to Walla Walla would take hours out of Mom or Dad's day.

"I'm happy for you to do it." Happy might have been too strong a word, but she was willing.

Adam gently removed the cast, his fingers capable and strong. Then he unwrapped the bandage around her hand. She couldn't bring herself to look as he studied her fingers. He gently moved one and she flinched.

"Still a bit tender, I see."

She nodded, keeping her eyes on the floor.

"The cuts are healing nicely. The surgeon said there are internal stitches in there that will dissolve by themselves, but these superficial stitches look ready to come out now."

"Okay." Her voice came out shaky.

Adam looked over at Brandon. "You mind holding her other hand? It shouldn't hurt—just a bit of a pulling feeling, but sometimes the fear is worse than the operation."

Jodie darted a look at Brandon. She remembered him and Josh laughing about her fear of needles when she'd last gone in for a vaccination. Brandon's gaze met hers and he pulled his chair over to sit beside her. He took her other hand in his, clasped their fingers together and rested them on his lap. Suddenly all she could think about was the feel of his hand holding hers, the way his mouth lifted in one corner, his eyes locked on hers.

"Distracted enough?" he whispered.

Um. Yes.

Something pulled in her hand and she let out a little gasp, jerking her head back toward Adam. Brandon's hand came to settle on her cheek, gently nudging her eyes back toward him.

"This way."

His hand was still grasping hers, firmly but gently. His work-roughened fingers slid down her face and she shivered involuntarily. He grinned.

What was he doing? She couldn't make sense of it. Couldn't feel anything but the warmth of his touch, couldn't see anything but the depth in his green eyes. Hadn't he said they were friends? Nothing more, nothing less?

Adam chuckled and tapped her arm. "I'm done. You can stop holding hands now." He gave Brandon a meaningful look. "If you want to."

Jodie pulled her fingers from Brandon's, face burning.

Adam's smile was mischievous as he looked at Brandon. "I don't think she felt any of that. You're a great … nurse."

Brandon laughed, but it sounded uncomfortable. No one spoke another word as Adam made her a splint for her hand to replace the cast. Jodie knew Brandon must be as embarrassed as she was. Thanks, Adam.

They walked out of the office as a girl was wheeling herself in.

"Jodie," Adam called after her. "Have you and Brandon met Arianne?"

Jodie glanced back at Adam, and then to the girl in the wheelchair again. "No." She held out her good hand. "I'm Jodie. And this is Brandon."

The girl smiled. "Arianne Rayne. Pleased to meet you."

She spoke cautiously, almost as though she expected Jodie to reject her or judge her in some way. Jodie held up her hand.

"Don't let Adam torture you too much. He's already had that pleasure with me."

Arianne laughed, and it was a nice sound.

Adam appeared at the door. "What are you saying about me?"

"The truth." Jodie grinned. "Nothing but the truth."

Adam rolled his eyes and grinned, then moved aside to let Arianne into the therapy room. "I'll see you next week, Jodie. And no doubt you too, Brandon."

Jodie avoided Brandon's eyes as he opened the door for her. Would he come? She hoped so.

"Arianne seems nice," she said for nothing better to say.

Brandon nodded. "They were talking about her at the gym. She was injured in a car accident."

Jodie saw the way his face paled and he went quiet. He was thinking about them. About his driving. He'd been so careful with his driving this morning, bringing her here. Not overly cautious, but smooth and gentle on the corners.

"Brandon," she said quietly. He looked at her. "Thank you."

A muscle in his jaw ticked, but he held her gaze. Then he dipped his head briefly as he opened his truck door for her.

So much meaning passed between them in that moment of silence. Neither spoke on their way to the sheriff's office. They didn't need to.

CHAPTER SEVENTEEN

Brandon was grateful for Jodie's company as they went to the county sheriff's office. He'd brought the order of service from Ariel's funeral with him.

Sheriff Thompson appeared gruff, but Brandon knew he was soft-hearted underneath. The sheriff had once caught him speeding and let him off with a warning. He came to the front counter as they entered his office.

"Brandon. I was sorry to hear about your mother. I hear it was a beautiful funeral service. I would have come if I wasn't on duty."

Brandon's heart warmed. "Thank you, sir."

Sheriff Thompson tapped the counter. "How can I help you?"

"Well, I'm looking for someone." Brandon put the order of service on the counter. "I want to get in contact with the Pereira family, but I don't want to travel all the way to Vancouver then find they've moved on."

"Vancouver, Washington?"

"Yes. And I don't like the idea of stalking them on social media. Do you know how I could get in touch with them?"

"Well now." Sheriff Thompson opened the order of service. "Even if they were in some kind of trouble with the law, I wouldn't be allowed to give out their details from my system." He grinned. "But I could stalk them on social media—just like you could."

Brandon glanced at Jodie. Maybe that was the way to go after all, as much as he didn't like the idea.

"How do you know them?" Sheriff Thompson asked.

"Their daughter—Ariel—was in my class at school."

"You lived in Vancouver?"

"Yes."

The sheriff studied the funeral sheet. He frowned. "The minister who performed the service, this Reverend Thomas Merrin, did you know him?"

"No, but Paige Merrin, the girl who gave the eulogy, was Ariel's best friend.'

Sheriff Thompson handed back the funeral sheet. "If you don't want to go the social media route, my advice would be to ask the church ministers in town." He looked at Jodie. "Your father, for a start. It's a small world, and believers are often interconnected. If that doesn't work, search online for church ministers, starting in Vancouver."

Brandon nodded. That felt a whole lot less like stalking someone. "Thank you so much. We'll do that."

The sheriff gave them a brief salute, then his eyes settled on Jodie's hand. "What happened to you?"

"Got it caught in a car door."

He winced. "Ouch."

Jodie grinned. "It was."

"Well, best of luck to you both." He nodded at them, then turned to Jodie. "And you look after yourself."

She nodded. "I will."

"I will too." Brandon met the sheriff's gaze to find a knowing smile on his face.

"I know you will, son. Good day."

————

BRANDON HELPED Jodie with her seat belt, then sat looking at her. She pointed to his phone.

"You going to call Dad?"

"Hmm. Yeah."

She grinned. "What are you waiting for?"

"I thought we should try Pastor Wilder from Trinity Lakes Community Church first."

"Okaay …"

"But I won't call him. We'll go in in person."

"Why?"

"Because someone needs to get to know people in this town." He gently picked up her splinted hand. "Someone needs to make new friends." He raised his eyebrows at her.

"You think I should make friends with the pastor from another church?"

"Yes. You need to check out the competition." His grin told her he knew how ridiculous his statement was.

"Fine. Let's do it."

He set her hand gently on her lap, then put his truck into gear. "Church on Main Street, here we come."

"You ever been there before?"

"Nah." He turned the corner. "Scary people there."

Jodie giggled. "I thought the Kennedys were your friends. And the Thomases. And your cousin Becky."

He widened his eyes in mock horror. "They go there? They don't come to our church? Why didn't anyone tell me they were the enemy?"

Jodie laughed, but she knew some Christians did take the fiery darts of the enemy and hurl them at fellow believers. And sometimes at themselves. God knew she'd been guilty of it herself. She'd used truth without love as a weapon, and poor Brandon had been in the firing line.

———

Pastor Dean Wilder invited them into his office with a smile as they introduced themselves.

"Call me Dean." He turned to face Jodie. "You're Theo Ladan's daughter, aren't you?"

She nodded and his smile grew ten degrees warmer. "I've got a lot of respect for your dad." He motioned them both to a seat in his office, then sat down too. "Now, how can I help?"

Brandon passed him Ariel's order of service. "Sheriff Thompson suggested you might know of the Reverend Thomas Merrin who officiated this funeral service."

"Merrin." Dean's brow furrowed. "I haven't heard of him, but I do know a Pereira family in Richland. I could ask them."

Jodie saw the way Brandon tensed, then fell back in his chair. "Not likely to be the same ones. Richland's only an hour away from here."

"I believe they lost a daughter many years ago." Dean tapped his chin. "And I believe they did come from Vancouver. After their daughter died, they moved to be closer to their married son. Samuel, I think his name is."

Could it be? Jodie glanced at Brandon. What was he thinking?

"How do you know them?" she asked Dean.

"I've met him a few times at church conferences. He's an elder in the church in Richland." Dean looked at Brandon, and his tone turned gentle, undemanding, but curious. "I'd be interested to know why you're looking for them."

Brandon blinked a couple of times and Jodie saw the way his chin trembled. She wanted to hold him. To hug him.

"Ariel is the reason I became a Christian. I have her Bible

and I want to return it and I want to tell the Pereiras what an impact Ariel had on my life."

Dean's eyes widened. "You're from Vancouver?"

"Originally, yes."

"So it would be the same family." He smiled. "How about I give them a call and see if they mind me passing on their details?" He handed the order of service back to Brandon. "I can look them up in my regional church directory."

"Now?" The paper shook in Brandon's hand.

"Yes. If you'd like me to."

Brandon glanced at Jodie and she saw the fear that passed through his eyes. She would have loved to take his hand or give him a reassuring pat on his shoulder, but her injured hand was closest to him and it would be obvious if she stood and went to his other side. Instead, she smiled at him and prayed.

Lord, give him peace. Guide this conversation. Help him, Lord.

He smiled back at her, then faced Dean. "I'd appreciate that."

Dean turned to his laptop and clicked a few buttons. "Here we are. Abraham Pereira." He took out his phone and tapped in the numbers.

Jodie held her breath. What if they were different people? Or worse, what if they didn't want to speak with Brandon?

Please Lord, please Lord ...

She didn't realize she'd been jiggling until Brandon reached over and placed a warm hand on her knee to make her stop. He grinned at her.

"You look more nervous than I am."

She rubbed a hand across her forehead. "Yeah. Sorry."

"Hello, Abraham?" They both turned as Dean spoke into his phone. "It's Pastor Dean Wilder from Trinity Lakes here. Yes, yes, I'm well. How are you doing?"

Jodie held her breath, waiting. Once the small talk was over, Dean tapped a pen on his desk.

"Abraham, I have a young man here in my office who'd like

to get in touch with you. He knew your daughter, and I think you'd like to hear what he has to say."

Brandon's hand on her knee tensed and Jodie reached over to clasp it.

"No, not today. I wondered if you'd like to come over here when you can. Meet in my office, maybe."

Brandon's hand relaxed and Jodie smiled at him.

"Tomorrow?" Dean raised his eyebrows at Brandon. He nodded. "Yes, tomorrow is good. Eleven o'clock? Perfect. I think your wife might like to come too. And any family members who might like to hear about the way God used Ariel in a young man's life." He laughed, joy filling his eyes. "Yes. I can't wait to hear the details either. Why do you think I suggested meeting here?"

Jodie couldn't stop her smile. It grew so wide it felt as though it would split her face. Brandon was biting his lip, still clearly nervous.

Dean hung up and beamed at them. "Tomorrow at eleven o'clock."

Brandon didn't seem to be able to talk.

"Thank you." Jodie stood. "Thank you so much, Pastor Dean."

Brandon stood too and Dean shook his hand. "God is good, brother, God is good."

Brandon wiped his hands down his jeans and nodded. "He is."

They hadn't even reached the car before Jodie threw her arms around him in a hug. She couldn't help herself. Brandon stopped in his tracks. Then his arms came around her waist and held her gently. He rested his head on the top of her hair and let out a long, slow breath.

"Thank you for being here," he whispered. "And thank you, God."

Jodie beamed. She'd never heard him openly talk to God

before. He avoided praying in public and had never seemed comfortable with it.

She stepped back and tugged at his hand. "You'd better take me home. My parents might think I've been kidnapped."

"Really?" He allowed her to drag him to the car. "Well, they might have to get used to it. I'm coming to kidnap you at ten-thirty tomorrow to pray with you before we come to the church."

Jodie's heart leapt. He wanted her there. At this life-changing time of his life, he wanted her there to share his joy and pain, to be his friend.

She laughed at him. "I don't think kidnapping will be necessary."

CHAPTER EIGHTEEN

Jodie was surprised to see the Junk Man's council vehicle pull up outside at ten thirty the following morning. She'd expected Brandon, not his father.

The passenger door of the truck opened and Brandon climbed out. He jogged up the front steps, and she dashed over to open the front door before he rang the bell. Her mouth went dry when he grinned at her. He was dressed in a new pair of jeans that fit him to perfection, and his shoulders filled out his blue shirt nicely.

"Been watching for me?"

"Maybe." Her cheeks heated. "Your dad's coming?"

"Yeah. I'm a bit nervous, so Dad offered to come. And I don't know if I'm safe to drive this morning. My head's all over the place." His gaze didn't leave hers and in it she saw humility and vulnerability.

"I trust you, Brandon."

He blinked, then slowly smiled. She found herself swallowing hard. Did he have any idea of the power of his smile?

"You still want to pray?" she asked.

"Here? Now?"

She nodded and he looked uncertain. "I'll pray if you like," she said. "I'll be quick."

He nodded and she took his hand in hers. He stared down at their clasped hands and she had to close her eyes. She wouldn't be able to concentrate on the prayer if she didn't.

"Lord, you know our hearts, you know all Brandon's been through. Lord, please give him courage today, give him the words to speak, and may it be a day of healing. For everyone. Bless him Lord, more than he ever imagined possible. Fill his life with good things. Amen."

She opened her eyes to find he was now looking directly at her, his green eyes glistening. She had to look away.

She tugged at his hand. "We'd better not keep your dad waiting. Let's go." She dropped his hand and pulled the door shut behind her.

"Yeah." He ran a hand through his hair and blew out a breath as he walked beside her to his dad's truck. "God, give me the words."

He opened the door for her and waited for her to settle into her seat and pass him the seat belt. He pulled it down and clicked it in. "Let's do this," he said before shutting her door and racing around to the front passenger seat.

The ride to the church was silent, and Jodie wondered if she should say something. But what? Luke never spoke much, and Brandon was clearly nervous. She looked down at her splinted hand. If her injury had never happened, she'd be in New York right now. She would have missed all this. For the first time, she thanked God for her injury, for the privilege of sharing this day with Brandon.

———

Pastor Wilder met them at the door.

He smiled and held out his hand to Dad. "Good morning. I'm Dean, and you're obviously Brandon's father."

Brandon breathed a sigh of relief. He hadn't been sure how the pastor would react to having the "Junk Man" in his church, especially with all the posters up around town.

Dad shook Dean's hand. "Yes, I'm Luke."

"Great to meet you, Luke." He looked at Brandon. "Come this way. Everyone's here."

They followed Dean into a side room. Comfortable couches circled the space, and a coffee table holding a plate of sandwiches sat in the middle of the room. The floor was covered by a warm-colored rug.

Brandon forced himself to look at the other people in the room. He saw Ariel in the faces of her family. They shone with that same joy and peace he'd been so attracted to in Ariel.

And it struck him. It wasn't Ariel he'd been attracted to. It was the love of Jesus in her.

He nodded at the young man who was obviously Ariel's brother. He had the same hair, the same skin tone. Then he looked at the young woman by his side and stopped.

"Paige?" Ariel's friend.

She smiled, but it was a cautious smile. "I married Samuel," she said softly.

Brandon swallowed a lump in his throat. He sat, trying to get comfortable. Not that there was anything comfortable about being here. Jodie sat on one side of him, his father on the other.

How much had Pastor Dean told them?

He looked at Ariel's parents. "I'm Brandon and I knew Ariel," he said. "She probably told you about me ... how I hassled her at school ..." Shame clouded his thoughts and he desperately searched for the right words.

Her parents gave the slightest nod, but he sensed no judgment in their expressions.

"Well." Brandon cleared his throat, then fingered the pages of

Ariel's Bible which he'd had clenched in his hands until now. "I wanted to return something of Ariel's."

He leaned forward and placed the Bible on the coffee table. Each member of the family sat perfectly still, every eye fixed steadfastly on him.

"I have my own now. And I know Jesus." He cleared his throat. "Thanks to Ariel and her journal entries."

Still no one moved. Brandon cleared his throat again, fighting against the roughness there. "I guess I just want to say thank you. Thank you for raising Ariel to be the godly young woman she was. Thank you for giving me her Bible, for allowing me to read her journal entries, to read her prayers for me, to help me see what a true relationship with Jesus looks like and what it means to walk with Him. I'm sad that it cost Ariel her life for me to see that. I'm sorry for what it cost her and your family." He looked at Paige. "And I'm sorry for all the times I mocked you and persecuted you for your faith."

A choking noise came from Ariel's mother. He looked at her, his own eyes burning.

"I thought I loved Ariel," he said, "but she loved me in the best way possible. I wanted her to belong to me, but she wanted me to belong to Jesus, to know Him and be in heaven one day." He swallowed hard. "And I will be. Because of her, I will be and I wanted you to know that." His throat felt rough. "And my mother will be, too."

"And so will I."

Brandon spun to face his father. Had he heard right? Dad put an arm around his shoulder.

"And so will I," he repeated, his eyes locking with Brandon's. "I saw the way your mother's life changed when she chose to believe. And I saw that in her dying months she was more alive than she'd ever been. God was in that room when she died. Jesus came to get her. She saw Him. I felt Him."

Brandon's chest heaved. His heart filled and his eyes spilled.

He dropped his head into his hands, overwhelmed, unable to speak. Around him he heard sniffles and quiet crying. Arms came around him from all sides and hands rested on his shoulders.

Oh God, you were doing so much more than I ever imagined. You are good. So good. I am in awe of you. Your love, your grace, your mercy.

He didn't realize he was praying out loud until an unfamiliar voice joined in. He opened his eyes and looked up. Ariel's father had his eyes shut tight, one hand on Brandon's shoulder, his other hand in the air, his face lifted to the sky.

"Father God, you didn't take our daughter's life. You don't take life, you multiply it. Ariel was a beautiful gift given for just the right amount of time, and we will see her again. We miss her, but how can we deny the joy of knowing that through taking her home, you have given us new brothers and sisters in Christ? You are the God of life. Of truth. Of love."

Goosebumps spread over Brandon's skin.

Speak life.

Speak truth.

Speak love.

How could he have wasted so many words for so many years? Carelessly used words that tore down and destroyed rather than built up? His heart was filled with a need to speak life. He waited until Ariel's family and Pastor Dean had finished praying, then he looked around at them all. Saw the red-rimmed eyes, but also the joy and life shining in them.

He knew he would never forget this moment. In fact, he didn't know near enough about God, but he suspected He'd allowed Ariel to look down from heaven and see this moment. He hoped so, anyway. If not, he'd certainly be telling her about it when he got to heaven.

CHAPTER NINETEEN

Jodie was surprised by how light-hearted Brandon was that afternoon. It was as though a huge weight had been lifted from his shoulders. Joy shone in his eyes.

His father had just dropped them off at his house, and Brandon had changed into casual jeans and a t-shirt.

He came to join her where she sat waiting for him on the front step. "Have you ever been rowing on the lake?" he asked as he lowered himself down beside her.

She shook her head.

"Right, that's it. We need to go rowing."

She laughed and held up her splinted hand. "And how am I going to do that?"

He held out his arms. "I have enough arms for both of us."

She giggled. "You identify as an octopus?"

He pulled a face, then flexed his muscles. "I mean I have enough muscles for both of us."

He did. She pushed one of his arms down. "Okay, okay. If you don't mind rowing for both of us …"

He stood and reached for her hand. "Not at all. We'll hire

one of those rowing dinghies Hannah Gilbertson has down there, and you can relax."

Relax when they were out on the lake, just the two of them, facing one another in a boat with him rowing? Relax was probably not the right word.

———

HANNAH EYED JODIE'S hand uncertainly. "You sure this is a good idea?"

Brandon grinned. "It's fine. I've got it."

"Hmm." Jodie wanted to laugh. Hannah did the doubting parent look so well. "You realize she has to get into the boat, which means having good balance?"

"I've got enough balance for both of us."

Both Jodie and Hannah laughed out loud, and Brandon shook his head.

"If you're worried, why don't you get someone to hold the boat steady while I help her in?"

Jodie put up her hand. "Do I get any say in this? I am right here."

Hannah laughed. "Brandon thinks a broken hand equates to a broken mouth." She turned her back on Brandon and faced Jodie. "What would you like to do?"

"Do you think I'd be safe if someone else held the boat steady while I get in?"

"Should be. You realize you've signed the safety waivers though? If anything happens …"

"Yeah. I know. It's on us, and so it should be." Jodie thought for a minute, then nodded. "I need to do this. I've lived here my whole life, and I've never been out on the lake."

Hannah's mouth dropped open, then she became all business.

"You're right. You need to do this. I'll see if Joel's around. He can help." She clicked her tongue and shook her head as she walked off. "Never been out on the lake," she muttered, her words fading as she stalked toward the rowing club.

Jodie giggled and turned back to Brandon. "Now she's got a bee in her bonnet."

Brandon grinned back and their eyes locked. Her mouth dried but she couldn't look away.

"It's a perfect day," she managed to say.

"Yeah." He stepped closer. "You sure you want to do this? I know I've been pressuring you, but if you don't feel it's safe … well, you've been right before."

She looked away. "I've also been insular and overprotective of myself and others. It's good that you're challenging me to step out of my comfort zone." Even better that he was doing it with her. "I saw you do it for Josh. I saw him come alive when he'd thought the accident had stolen his hopes and dreams. Now look at him. Studying in Bible college, engaged, reaching out."

"And living a life apart from me." Brandon gave a self-deprecating laugh. "I'm like a parent watching their child leave home and not wanting to let go."

She stared at him. Would it be the same with her? Would he want to help her, encourage her, challenge her, and then let her go?

"Here they come." He pointed to Hannah and Joel coming from the rowing club, side by side.

Jodie's heart squeezed. How she'd love that to be her and Brandon someday. But just like he had done with Josh, she needed to let him go. But not today. Today she would enjoy his company, enjoy his smiles, enjoy his attention, enjoy everything about him.

Joel grinned at Jodie. "Ready for a new adventure, I hear." He slapped Brandon on the back. "Don't know that I'd be trusting this one, but that's up to you."

Brandon rolled his eyes, but Jodie knew he wasn't upset. The shine of joy never left his eyes. Joel held one end of the boat while Brandon stepped in. He looked so steady on his feet. So strong. Capable.

Hannah took Jodie's arm and held her firm. Jodie looked at the boat gently swaying on the water. Suddenly the water looked deep, the boat unsteady.

Brandon reached out an arm and smiled at her. "I feel like we're doing a reverse Jesus and Peter." His expression softened, became tender. "Come to me," he said, his tone gentle and encouraging. "Keep your eyes on me, not the water."

A laugh caught in her throat. She reached her injured hand out to him and he grasped it firmly at the elbow. She put one foot in and the boat rocked. She gasped.

Before she knew what had happened, both his arms came around her waist and he lifted her into the boat and held her close. She stared up at him, not daring to speak until Hannah and Joel had the boat steady again.

She pushed back from him. "What happened to the whole 'come to me, Jesus' thing?"

He grinned. "I'm not as patient as Jesus." He held her arms and lowered her into the seat of the boat.

"Hey, mate," Joel said, "How about a heads up if you're going to do something like that?"

Brandon's smile dimmed. "Sorry."

Jodie stared at him. Since when did Brandon apologize?

"Yeah, all good." Joel stepped back from the boat. "You two have a great time. It's a beautiful day."

"Yeah. Thanks." Brandon lifted one hand from the oars Hannah had passed him and waved. Then he began to row. Jodie watched his arms, fascinated. He moved the oars through the water with ease, as though he'd done it many times before.

"Hey," She looked up to see an amused smile on his lips.

"You're supposed to be looking out at the beauty of God's creation."

She was. There was certainly beauty in the way the tendons in his forearms moved, the way his broad shoulders tightened and released with each movement of the oars. She bit her lip and smiled, forcing herself to look out across the water to other parts of God's creation, like the mountains in the distance. The view was magnificent from here. And peaceful. She'd walked along the edge of the lake many times, but out here, with just her and Brandon and God, it was peaceful in a way that filled her soul.

They didn't speak much, but she felt Brandon's eyes on her many times. Sometimes she'd peek at him again and his lips would tug up in a half smile. She'd once feared that smile. Feared the smug, amused look that meant he was making fun of someone. But today it was different. There was a tenderness there. An understanding and connection filled with respect and … well, love might be too strong a word, but something close.

"I wish I was able to row," she finally said, her voice breaking the stillness, the gentle swishing of the waves.

He pulled a face. "I don't know that you do. Did Josh tell you about the first time I took him rowing?"

"No. What happened?"

"I might have deliberately rowed against him."

"Might have?" She sputtered out a laugh. "You did."

"Yeah. Well, he was so competitive. Wanted us to time each other from one side of the lake to the other. We both had a set of oars, and I didn't want him to get too big-headed, so …"

Jodie laughed. "You two are as bad as each other."

Brandon's smile faded. "If I'm honest, I do miss him. I mean, I'm happy for him and I know it's right that he has Hallie and that he's studying at college, but we had a lot of good times."

"I know." She'd heard them. The shouts of laughter as they'd played video games together in the basement, the banter they shared as they nudged and jostled each other, the shared looks, the fun. She'd envied them. And feared them. She didn't want to become an object of their ridicule.

"There are definitely some good changes though," Brandon said as though reading her thoughts. "I'm definitely not proud of the way we used to stir each other up and mock people."

"I used to preach at you, and I'm not proud of that."

His eyes fastened on hers. Then he smiled.

"It's all turned out kind of nicely though, hasn't it?"

"What do you mean?"

"I mean, we get to share all this together." His eyes took in the lake around them, then focused back on her. "Now Josh is out of the picture, I get to spend time with his sister."

"And I get to spend time with his best friend." She grinned at him. "I'm not too upset about it."

"But you could have been at NYU." She heard the uncertainty in his tone.

"I could have been. But I would've missed being here for you when your mom died. I would've missed seeing the miracle of today, hearing the story of how you came to know Jesus. I would have missed ..." She met his eyes. "I would have missed you."

He looked away, and her heart sank. She'd said too much. Made him uncomfortable. He turned and rowed back toward the jetty.

Oh Lord. Her heart hurt. She bit her lip and focused on the shoreline, the warmth of the day no longer bringing the same joy.

Joel and Hannah were waiting. Joel held the boat while Hannah reached her hands out for Jodie. Brandon stood and held her other arm, supporting her as she stepped onto the jetty. Brandon followed.

"Will you be back?" Hannah asked with a grin.

"Of course." Jodie smiled, though her heart was heavy. "It's beautiful out there. I can't believe it's taken me this long to do it."

"Me either." Hannah shook her head. "Me either."

———

THEY WALKED in silence back to Brandon's truck. He opened the passenger door and helped her with her seat belt.

"Brandon?"

He stopped, his face inches from hers as he clicked her seat belt into place. "Yeah?"

"I'm sorry if I made you uncomfortable. I was speaking the truth, but maybe it wasn't helpful. Maybe I was—"

"I would have missed you, too."

She stared at him. His mouth was inches from hers, his captivating green eyes fixed on her lips. He looked up to meet her gaze and smiled.

She drew in a breath and he moved closer, his eyes searching hers. He must have seen the hope amidst the fear. His lips touched hers in a brief, gentle kiss. Then he smiled into her eyes.

"Sometimes I miss you when I'm in the same room as you. When I'm by your side. Everything in me wants you closer. Wants more."

"Oh, Brandon." Her heart swelled and tears filled her eyes.

"Hey, it's okay."

She laughed and sniffled. "I know. It's just I ... I can't quite believe it. After all this time trying to hide my feelings, having to fight the attraction—"

She cut herself off. She hadn't meant to say that. Hadn't meant to reveal the deepest desires of her heart.

His eyes crinkled in the corners as he smiled. "You're saying you have feelings for me? I didn't think you'd ever consider me, reckless, immature, insensitive man that I was."

Lord? How much should she tell him? *Speak the truth in love.* Not speaking would be fear holding her back. It would be self-protection. Brandon needed to know the truth.

"I didn't just consider you. I dreamed of you. I hoped. Prayed." She blushed. "I tried to kid myself I didn't feel anything, but deep down ..."

He unclipped her seat belt and reached for her hand. "We can't have this conversation here. Come on." He held out his hand and she took it. He led her to the nearby picnic table and sat down, pulling her down beside him.

He turned sideways on the bench to face her and grinned. "Now, keep telling me how much you love and adore me."

She laughed and swatted his arm, her shoulders relaxing. This was Brandon. Her friend. God's child. She didn't need to fear being honest with him.

"I'm done," she said.

"Well, I'm not." He moved closer and his thigh pressed against hers. "Not nearly done." His hand came up to rest on the side of her head, his thumb caressed her face. "I think you are the prettiest, most gracious, most godly girl I've ever known. I didn't dare dream you'd ever see me as more than your brother's immature friend. Didn't dare dream I'd ever be worthy of you. You're a pastor's daughter. A Ladan."

She smiled. "And you're God's child. Son of the King of the Universe."

His Adam's apple bobbed. "Yeah." His smile tipped. "Does that mean it's okay for me to kiss you? Properly?"

"Um." Her heart pounded double time. She'd dreamed of this. Longed for this. "Yes," she whispered.

He smiled. A full, complete smile. Then his hands came up to gently cradle her face and he kissed her. Every sense came alive and warmth filled her as her arms involuntarily came around him. She had never kissed anyone before, didn't know how to, but his gentle exploration of her lips encouraged her, prompted her to press deeper. She felt as though her body was on fire, as senses she didn't know she possessed came alive. Overwhelmed, she pulled back.

Brandon was breathing hard, his gaze fixed on hers, questioning.

"Sorry. I just … wow."

He smiled and nodded. "Yeah."

"Does that make us … are we a couple?"

He laughed. "I think it does."

She bit her lip. What did that mean exactly? And what about the future? She had no idea what she'd be doing once her hand healed.

Trust me.

She smiled. No more self-protection. God held her future and she could trust Him no matter what.

Brandon reached for her hand, and she placed it in his warm one. He led her back to his truck. He leaned over her to do up her seat belt again, paused to touch his lips to hers then smiled into her eyes.

"As much as I enjoy this, I'm looking forward to you getting rid of that splint."

"Why?"

He pulled a face. "It kind of poked into me when you had your arms around me." He stepped back and rubbed a spot on his back. "I didn't notice it at the time, but I can feel it now."

"Brandon, I'm sorry."

He tucked a wisp of her hair behind her ear. "Don't be sorry. It was totally worth it." Then he closed her door and went around to the driver's side.

CHAPTER TWENTY

Brandon sat in the back row of church, Jodie by his side. He grinned and held her hand. She grinned back.

Josh and Hallie moved into the row in front of them. "Hey, have you met my girlfriend?" Brandon held up their clasped hands.

Hallie's eyes widened, and Josh grinned. "About time."

"Yeah, I reckon." Jackson Reilly stopped on his way down the aisle and rolled his eyes. "Seriously, we were all getting tired of waiting."

Jodie laughed. "Hey, come on. As if you knew."

"Everybody knew." Ellie Reilly had stopped too. "That whole love-hate thing you had going on? It was so obvious."

Brandon frowned. Were they for real?

The aisle was getting crowded as Jasper joined the gathering, along with Jocelyn and Dylan.

"I knew when they had that little—what did Lexi call it?— biffo at Hallie and Josh's engagement party," Jackson said. "It didn't escape my notice that Jodie couldn't keep her eyes off his chest."

"I was worried because I thought I'd—"

"I knew way before that," Jocelyn cut in, looking at Brandon. "You remember that day we got a callout for your mother?" Brandon remembered back to that day. Mom had fainted, a result of the as-yet undiagnosed cancer. "Jodie only had eyes for you. I saw the love and compassion there."

"Hey," Jodie said.

"I knew way before that." Ellie waved a hand at Jocelyn. "I remember the first day Brandon came to church. Jodie was still in high school. I saw the way she kept glancing at him. I don't think she heard a word of the sermon."

Josh laughed. "Come on, guys. People are trying to get past you. Let's let Jodes and Brando live in their own little delusional world, thinking they've surprised us." He widened his eyes in mock surprise. "Oh, guys, I never saw that coming. Wow. Congratulations!"

"Yeah, congratulations." Jackson said with a laugh. "I hope it lasts, what with it being so unexpected and you two so not being the perfect match and all."

Their laughter drowned out anything else that might have been said, and Brandon grinned. What were friends for if not to have fun at your expense? He deserved it after all the times he'd messed with them.

"Excuse me, but can we clear the aisle?" Old Mr. Carrigan shuffled through and everyone went to find a seat as the worship band played their pre-service song.

Jodie was blushing.

She gave him a shy smile. "Well, I wasn't expecting that kind of attention."

"Me either." He froze. A familiar figure had come in the door, all dressed up and looking self-conscious. "Dad?"

His father's face filled with relief. "There you are. I almost called to ask you to pick me up, but I didn't want to intrude." He looked between Jodie and Brandon and smiled.

Brandon laughed. "We wouldn't have minded."

"Definitely not." Jodie slid along the row to make room.

"Good. Because I'm feeling like a fish out of water. Haven't been in a church for years, except for funerals."

Like his mother's. Familiar sadness welled up, but it was bittersweet. Mom was in heaven waiting for him, and Dad was here with him in church.

Pastor Ladan began the service and Brandon settled in to listen, his heart full. He didn't hear much of the service. He was too distracted by Jodie's hand in his and the way his father sat in rapt attention, soaking up every word Theo Ladan spoke.

JODIE FELT proud of the way church members greeted Brandon's father with a nod and a smile after the service. No one overwhelmed him or smothered him with attention the way they did with some newcomers, but neither did they ignore him.

"You coming to join us at Joe's?" Josh asked from where he stood in the row in front of them, his arm around Hallie.

Jodie looked at Brandon. "You want to?"

"Not today." He nodded toward his dad.

Jodie glanced at Luke. Of course. They shouldn't abandon him and she couldn't imagine him agreeing to come to Joe's Diner. He was a quiet man. Strong and dependable, but a bit of a loner.

"You two can go," Luke said. "I'd like to stay behind and ask your dad some questions."

"Why don't you both come to our house for lunch?" Jodie asked. "I'll check with Mom, but I know she'll be fine with it. She's always ready for unexpected visitors on a Sunday."

She looked up to see Dad making his way down the aisle toward them. He shook hands with Luke.

"Great to see you. How are you?"

"Doing well thanks, Pastor Theo."

"Can they come for lunch today?" Jodie cut in. "The Junk … Mr. McAffrey, Brandon's father—"

"Luke," Brandon's father said with a grin.

She blushed. "Luke has some things he'd like to discuss with you."

Brandon grinned at her. "You realize my dad has a tongue of his own?"

Jodie blushed again and looked apologetically at Luke.

"It's fine." Luke smiled at her, a smile so like Brandon's she couldn't help smiling back.

"You're very welcome to come for lunch," Dad said, looking at Luke. "And we can always go into my study for privacy if that helps." He shot an amused look at Jodie.

"No, no," Luke shook his head. "What I have to say involves Jodie and Brandon too."

What? Jodie darted a look at Brandon. He shrugged back at her. Now she was nervous.

Brandon squeezed her hand. "Don't worry. Dad's not as scary as he looks."

"He looks exactly like you."

"As I said…" He leaned over and kissed her on the cheek. "Not scary at all. In fact, a very handsome man if you ask me."

Jodie laughed and bumped her shoulder against his, but she couldn't disagree.

———

BRANDON WAS glad Theo Ladan didn't push his father to speak as they ate lunch in the Ladan home. He'd learned his father never wasted time on empty words and always spoke in his own time.

They had almost finished lunch when Dad looked down at his phone. "I've marked those verses you were talking about today, Theo," he said. He sat his phone on the table.

Guiltily, Brandon acknowledged he hadn't heard much of today's sermon. He'd been too focused on the pleasure of Jodie's presence beside him, imagining what it would be like to have her holding his hand every Sunday, perhaps sitting with a few little girls and boys who looked like both of them.

"I'm sure you're aware of the rumors about me going around town," Dad said.

Theo nodded. "I am."

"Well, 2 Corinthians 10 makes me think Paul was a bit like me. Timid at times on the things he chooses to let go, but bold when needed. I know some people see gentleness and humility as weakness, but they're wrong. I could've made a lot of trouble over the years, but I've held my peace. I've been hesitant to be bold about some things because I wasn't sure my motives were right, but that verse today about demolishing strongholds … well, it made me realize it's demolition day."

Brandon's eyes widened. "Demolition day?"

"There have been lies and pretension for a long time." Dad sighed and rubbed a hand over his forehead. "You heard Mariah's story. I wanted to let it go. Didn't want to stir anything up. But now I have Susannah Gilbertson spreading lies to hide the truth. She's threatened to have me evicted, buy my house, and demolish it."

Heat filled Brandon's chest. How dare she?

"I know Tabby Thomas has applied to have the boathouse rezoned. As it should be. But that was over a year ago and nothing has been approved yet. It's taking way too long." Dad tapped his fingers on the tablecloth. "People are starting to catch wind of the truth. That's what concerns me. Partial truth is open to being twisted." He sat up taller and looked at Theo. "That land by the lake has become a stronghold of the enemy. We need to pray. You said today that dependence on God is the greatest weapon. He will fight for us. With us."

Jodie's mouth had dropped open and Brandon was sure his

had too. Everyone was staring at his father. Brandon had never heard his father say so much. And he spoke like a man who knew Scripture. Who understood it.

"Dad?" Brandon didn't know exactly what he wanted to ask. How to ask.

Dad seemed to understand. He gave a wry smile. "I grew up in the church. My mom was a strong believer."

Brandon swallowed hard. There was so much he didn't know about his father. His family.

Dad looked at Brandon. "Did you say you were going to get Jodie to write an article for the paper, to get the truth out there?" He glanced at Jodie and she nodded. "Well, I think it's time. We need to demolish this stronghold—with truth and God's help."

"And love," Jodie said. "Speak the truth in love."

"Exactly." Dad nodded. "I didn't want to speak out earlier because it would have been revenge, and I despise that kind of weakness. I also didn't want to hurt people, but they're going to be hurt more if we don't speak out. It's demo day. Time to demolish every lie of the enemy. Wayne Gilbertson isn't the enemy. Susannah isn't, either. We have one adversary and God will help us defeat him."

Brandon sat back in his chair. Wow.

Jodie grinned. "Looks like we're going to war." She held up her injured hand. "I might not be fully functional, but David defeated Goliath with a little stone didn't he?"

Brandon put his arm around her. "I'll help you."

Lil Ladan looked between them all with wide eyes and Brandon fought the urge to laugh. Is this how David felt when he went out to fight Goliath? Hugely underequipped, but backed up by the biggest, most dependable hero ever—God Himself.

Pastor Theo took out a notebook, then set down his pen. "First, let's pray."

Brandon's mind swam as Pastor Theo prayed for wisdom, direction, humility, truth, and love.

Brandon took notes for Jodie as Dad shared his side of the story.

"I have all the paperwork supporting the original decision," he said. "I know Wayne Gilbertson may have benefited from the rezoning of the land, but I believe he genuinely wanted to save the town. I didn't want him to get into trouble. In hindsight …"

"No," Jodie said, and all eyes turned to her. She blushed faintly. "If there's one thing I've learned recently, it's that God's timing is perfect. He uses even our mistakes, our failings, for good if we turn everything over to Him. He's got this."

Dad grinned at her, then turned to Brandon. "You've got a good one here."

Brandon grinned back. "I know."

CHAPTER TWENTY-ONE

Jodie reread her article. After a week of writing and re-writing it was finally ready to be submitted to Trinity Lakes Gazette. She was sure Selena would be more than happy to print it.

"Dad's going to give all the original zoning paperwork to Tabby." Brandon said. "And the council."

"I thought Logan already submitted rezoning paperwork to the council for Tabby." Tabby's boyfriend Logan Wylde seemed to know what he was doing.

"He did." Brandon frowned. "But it's been nearly a year since Tabby submitted the rezoning application. Dad thinks something's fishy."

"Hopefully this will help." Jodie held up her article.

"Yeah. But … I feel like …"

Jodie waited, wanting to smooth out the furrow in his brow. "Like what?"

"I know I asked you to write the article, but I feel like the right thing to do is to meet with Tabby and Logan since they submitted the zoning request, as well as Hannah, Becky, Wayne, and maybe even Susannah, first. Give them the heads-up. We're not doing this to bring people down. We're doing this to fight for truth and justice."

A burden rolled from Jodie's shoulders. "I totally agree with you. I was feeling unsettled, and that's exactly why. How about we talk with your dad and my dad and see what we can arrange?"

———

"Sounds like a God-inspired idea to me," Jodie's dad said when she told him what she and Brandon had been discussing. "I'll see what I can do to get everyone together. Maybe I'll leave Susannah out of it. We don't need drama. We need to be heard."

Jodie nodded. Susannah had sliced Brandon's father's cheek with her ring a few months back. It was the reason the Junk Man had lost his trademark scraggly beard. The hospital had shaved him to stitch him up.

"Hannah could always tell her mother what we discussed after the meeting," Jodie agreed. "Or Wayne could tell her."

Her dad chuckled. "I don't think Wayne and Susannah go anywhere near each other these days. For good reason."

"Then we'll ask Hannah to tell her."

"Sounds like a plan. Let's make some phone calls."

———

On Sunday afternoon, Brandon looked around at the people crowded into the Ladans' living room for the meeting. What would Mom think of all this if she was still here? He suspected she would have enjoyed the drama. He, on the other hand, was nervous.

Hannah looked on edge too. Her eyes widened when she saw Brandon and his dad. People were used to his father being the quiet, invisible Junk Man who kept to himself.

"I know you're all wondering what this is about," Theo Ladan said, using his firm but calm pastor's voice, the one that had Brandon trusting him from the first day they'd met. "A lot of prayer and thought has gone into this meeting, and we need you all to feel free to speak openly with us, the way we are going to with you." He looked around. "We had hoped Wayne could make it, but perhaps Becky and Hannah, can pass on what's discussed."

A nervous look passed between Becky and Hannah, and Brandon felt for them. Becky had always made a special effort to make him feel included, despite her mom's order to keep her distance. He didn't want Becky hurt.

"Logan and Tabby, I believe you put in a request for rezoning of the land around the boathouse?" Pastor Ladan said.

Logan nodded. "That was in May last year. We're still waiting for the council to process the application."

"Luke may have some information that could help push it along." Pastor Ladan gestured toward Brandon's dad who nodded and passed over a pile of papers.

"These are the original land reports from twenty-five years ago. I'll email you copies later."

Everyone's eyes shot to Brandon's dad as though they'd never heard him speak before.

Logan glanced through the papers. "Where'd you get these?"

"From the council. Before I was the Junk Man, I was the council's developmental and planning officer. The lake isn't a flood zone. Never has been. But Wayne wanted it zoned that way to stop a developer coming in and changing the heart of our town. Of course we all wanted that, but I didn't think it was right to change the records."

He looked at Brandon. His turn. Brandon drew in a deep breath. *God give me the words. In truth and love.* "My mom made a confession before she died." He licked suddenly dry lips, taking courage when Jodie squeezed his hand. "She was Dad's girlfriend when he was on the council. She tried to convince Dad to doctor the records for Wayne, to show the area as a floodplain. The deal was, Wayne would get her a job at the council if she could do it." He glanced at his father, pride in his eyes. "Dad refused. His integrity wouldn't let him."

"Wait!" Hannah's eyes were flashing. "What exactly are you accusing my father of doing?"

Pastor Ladan gave her a gentle look. "I know this is all hard to listen to, but if you can hear us out."

Hannah fell quiet, but she didn't sit back. Her hands were clenched on her knees. Brandon knew how she felt. He knew how he'd felt when he'd learned the truth.

"Mom drugged Dad with sleeping pills so he'd miss the meeting." He swallowed the lump in his throat. "Wayne submitted fake reports."

Hannah gasped and Dad took over. "It's true. Some people made a fuss about me not being at the meeting, not doing my job properly. In the end, Wayne came to me. He had two choices. Fire me, or let the truth come out and have the land sold to a developer who wanted to ruin our town with over-priced lakefront apartments." Dad's expression was sympathetic as he looked at Hannah. "He's not a bad man. I know he bought the land once it was rezoned and got it cheaper because of it, but his purpose was to protect it. To protect the town. I wanted that too, so I told him that as long as he gave me some kind of work, I would take the fall."

Murmurs went around the room and a strangled cry came from Tabby. "I knew you were a hero. I knew it."

All eyes turned to her. She pointed at Brandon's father. "The Junk Man saved my sister. We went out in kayaks, and Tiffy fell out. Years ago. He dived into the lake and saved her. He never said a word. We didn't say anything because we shouldn't have been out there and didn't want to get into trouble."

Brandon looked at his dad whose green eyes were twinkling as he said, 'I thought that might be the case."

Brandon's respect for his father grew even more. "I had no idea."

Becky nodded. "I know. You used to degrade him all the time." Her hand flew to her mouth.

Brandon gave a lopsided smile. "It's okay. Dad and I have talked about it. My mom encouraged me to look down on Dad. To call him the Junk Man—"

"And worse," his dad cut in, but he was smiling.

"Yes. Mom was scared I'd find out he's my father. She left town as soon as she found out she was expecting me and went to Vancouver. We came back five years ago, and I got an apprenticeship at Trinity Auto. Once she was diagnosed with cancer she told me the truth." He looked at Theo. "Pastor Ladan has some of it recorded on his phone."

Tabby shook her head, tears glistening in her eyes. "So what now?"

Dad spoke up. "We're not out to cause trouble. We just want the truth to be known."

Brandon looked at Hannah and Becky. Both were pale, their expressions tense. "I know how you feel. I know how I felt when Mom told me the truth, anyway. The last thing we want is to hurt you or affect your dad's reputation. But your mom is forcing our hands. She's trying to get Dad evicted from his house. Making up rumors ..."

"I know." Becky bit her lip.

"But that's not on you."

"I can talk to Mom." Hannah spoke quickly. She sounded panicked. "I can tell her to back off. If it all comes out, she'll be in the firing line."

"Hannah, that won't work." Becky looked distressed. "You know what Mom's like."

Defeat slumped her shoulders.

"We don't want to hurt anybody," Pastor Ladan said. "We just believe it's time for the truth to be known. Jodie has written an article which she is going to submit to the Trinity Lakes Gazette. We've got a copy for each of you here. We don't want it to come as a shock to you, and we welcome your feedback. We want to speak the truth in love. No more secrets. No more strongholds of deceit."

There was complete silence as the copies were passed around. Hannah's hands were shaking and so were Jodie's. Was Jodie nervous about the content of the article, or the reactions to her work? Brandon knew she had nothing to be worried about. She was a gifted writer. She'd make an excellent journalist. He'd enjoyed helping her master text-to-speech the way he had helped Josh. It might even help her in her future career as a journalist. His heart sank. She deserved to go to NYU. Maybe there would still be a way when her hand healed. He wanted her to be happy. No matter what.

***

"THIS IS QUITE THE STORY, JODIE." Logan looked up from the article. "You wrote it?"

Jodie bit her lip and nodded. Their reactions mattered. She'd put heart and soul into it. "Brandon, Luke, and Dad helped with the details I wasn't sure of, like how the zoning works."

"She's a gifted writer," Brandon said, pride in his voice. "Did you know she had a scholarship to NYU? But her hand ..." His voice trailed off.

"Really?" Logan's eyes lit up. "You should see if Selena will take you on. She's always looking for more staff."

Jodie laughed. "I'm not qualified. Not yet, anyway."

Hannah looked up from the article. "You haven't actually said my dad doctored anything. You make him look like he was helping the town."

"He was, in his own way Although he could have handled it more ethically."

"But people know he was the mayor. Aren't they going to assume he doctored the records?"

"Maybe, but this article should help them understand why. I don't think anyone's going to begrudge him the land by the lake when he saved us from development. Besides, he gave you that land, didn't he?"

Hannah nodded.

Jodie looked at Luke, then back to Hannah. "Thanks to your dad, and thanks to Luke's care, we have a beautiful, well-kept piece of land where wildlife can live in relative safety. Instead of high-rise apartments."

"And my mom wants to make trouble." Becky looked at Luke. "She wants to bring you down, take away the haven you've made for the birds, and demolish your house."

Luke nodded. "That about sums it up."

Becky stood. "Print it." She looked at her sister. "Hannah?"

Hannah rubbed her forehead, then looked at Jodie. "It's missing one thing." Everyone waited. Hannah looked at Tabby, then at Luke. "The rescue. It should include you rescuing Tiffy."

Luke shrugged. "It's not my secret. You need to ask Tabby."

Tabby bit her lip, then smiled. "Put it in. I'm sick of it being a secret. It's not like Dad's going to ground me seventeen years later." She looked at Luke. "Thank you. You saved Tiffy's life that day."

"You're welcome." He chuckled. "It was a miracle I was there at just the right time. I thought I was in charge of my own life, my own movements, but God had me even back then." He grinned. "Not that I'm complaining."

"None of us are." Becky looked at Jodie and held up the article. "Can I show this to my mom?"

Jodie winced. "Maybe not until it's on its way to print. I don't want Selena threatened."

Becky's mouth drooped. "Yeah. I'm sorry, guys. Sorry for everything."

"Hey," Brandon said. "That's on your parents, not you. I've had to learn the same thing. I believed so many lies from my mom, picked up so many bad attitudes and habits, but today is demo day. We are demolishing the strongholds of the past."

"In God's strength," Dad added in his pastor's voice and stood. "And on that note, let's all pray."

Everyone stood and there in a circle together they committed Trinity Lakes, past, present, and future, into God's hands.

CHAPTER TWENTY-TWO

Jodie watched Selena read the article. Her face was unreadable.

Brandon nudged Jodie with his shoulder and gave an encouraging nod. He was the one who should be nervous. This story openly told the truth about his mother's betrayal. But also her conversion.

Finally Selena looked up. "I think you're an answer to prayer."

"I am?" Confused, Jodie looked from Selena back to Brandon.

"I've been looking into the zoning of the lakefront," Selena put the paper down on the desk. "Tabby Thomas asked me to look because the council kept brushing her off. She wants to develop the boathouse but it's affected by the zoning. So my investigations began with *Why are the council so slow?* and then, when I hit roadblocks at every turn, morphed into *What's with the zoning?* Only a few days ago, I finally placed it all in God's hands. Asked him to help me because to be honest, I'm exhausted. Writer's block is becoming a big problem for me. My other full-time writer left and I haven't been able to replace her. I can't write so well under pressure." She tapped the paper on her desk. "But you … you are a writer."

"But I haven't studied. I was going to go to NYU and study journalism, but …" Jodie held up her splinted hand.

Selena smiled. "Yeah, Logan told me what happened. Would you consider an apprenticeship instead? With me?"

Really? Jodie couldn't speak. Something like a squeak came out.

Brandon grinned down at her. "Is that a yes?"

Selena's eyes lit with hope. "You could ease in slowly as your hand heals. Work part time, study part time. There's plenty of on-line journalism courses." She pointed to the article. "You understand the heart of this town. You feel its heartbeat. And you have a way with words."

"Um." Jodie's heart was beating double-time. "Well, there's no guarantee I'll regain full use of my hand."

Selena grinned. "That's an excuse and you know it. Technology is a wonderful thing."

Jodie's mind raced, her thoughts unable to settle. Doubts prodded her. What if this was a one-off? What if God had helped her write this article but he didn't come to the party on her next one? Or the next? What if she suffered from writer's block too?

Demo day.

She wasn't sure if Brandon whispered, or if she just thought she heard it. No more lies. No more deceit. No more listening to the enemy. Fear and doubt were not from God. His words were strong, sure, full of life, truth, and love.

"I'll pray about it then get back to you," she said.

"Thank you." Selena beamed.

"What about this article. Will you print it?"

"Yes. And I'll put your name on it. Are you ready though?

Trinity Lakes is going to be in an uproar. You've opened a can of worms."

Brandon laughed. "Plenty of fish in the lakes to eat them. Let's hope they're tasty."

"The fish or the worms?"

"Both."

———

SELENA HAD BEEN RIGHT. Tuesday morning after Memorial Day, Rhonda Ingalls and her sister-in-law Marla arrived on Jodie's doorstep with the local paper containing Jodie's article.

"Is it true?" Marla demanded, waving the Gazette in Jodie's face.

Jodie laughed and took a step back.

"Of course it's true." Rhonda glared at her sister-in-law. "I told you there was something going on with that lakefront. And I always knew the Junk Man was a hero."

Jodie held back another laugh. "Would you like to come in? I'd make you a cup of coffee, but I'm likely to spill it on you."

"How did you injure your hand?" Rhonda asked as they walked past her and settled into the living room. Jodie shut the front door behind them.

"Got it caught in a car door." Change of subject needed. "Now you had some questions about the article?"

"No, no. The article is self-explanatory." Rhonda glared at her sister-in-law again. "But there is something I've been wondering about."

Jodie waited. What now? No one ever knew what Rhonda was going to come out with. She was known as the town gossip, but she didn't mean to meddle. She did genuinely have a good heart. She just didn't always have the full truth before she told it. And the love was sometimes forgotten.

"I hear that you and that McAffrey boy have been spending a lot of time together."

"You mean Brandon? Brandon Taylor?"

"The Junk Man's son."

Jodie nodded. "Yes, he had some time off work after his mother's death so he's been helping me. I hadn't realized what a handicap an injured hand would be. In fact, he's taking me to my PT appointment this morning to get my splint off. He'll be back at work tomorrow though."

Rhonda looked at Marla. "I told you I saw her coming out of Adam Lancaster's office with him."

Marla huffed, clearly put out that Rhonda had known something before she had.

Jodie tried not to laugh.

"We had an idea," Rhonda said, ignoring Marla's look. "That Gilbertson woman is going on about how the mess in the Junk Man's yard attracts mice and rats and that his geese are a problem."

Jodie nodded.

"Well, Marla and I want to start up a fundraiser and a community work day. We think we could get the townspeople to come together and make state of the art pens for his geese. Maybe even a pond in his yard. See, look, I found this." She held a printed piece of paper out for Jodie.

Jodie turned it around to look. It appeared to be some kind of plan for a temperature-controlled building housing rodent-proof aviaries.

"He could rehabilitate his animals in there," Marla said.

"It could go in his back yard and he could keep it nice and warm," Rhonda added, warming to the subject. "Even the pond could be heated. He could swim with his geese if he wanted to."

Jodie worked hard not to laugh. Speak of warming to the subject.

Marla let out a snort. "He doesn't need to go swimming with his geese."

"What if he has orphaned ones that need to learn to swim?" Rhonda looked hurt.

"They do that instinctively. Seriously Rhonda,—"

"I think it's a great idea," Jodie cut in. "I think we should talk to Brandon and his dad about it."

Rhonda beamed and Marla rolled her eyes. "She's talking about the rodent-proof aviaries, not the heated duck pool, Rhonda."

"I'm talking about all of it. Look, here's Brandon now. He's taking me to my appointment, but how about we meet again and discuss it more?"

Marla and Rhonda stood. Rhonda grabbed her paper back up from the couch and waved it at Jodie.

"So you confirm everything in here's true?"

Jodie nodded. "I do."

Rhonda let out a giggle of delight. "I heard it first from the source."

Jodie laughed too. She couldn't help it. She ushered the ladies out the door as Brandon came up the steps. He gave her a questioning look, but she shook her head and kept laughing.

———

"CAN you touch your index finger to your thumb?" Adam demonstrated the movement.

Jodie did so and winced.

"A bit of pain is normal. Your muscles and tendons need to get used to working again."

"You think I'll get full use back?"

Adam nodded. "Most likely. The plates and screws in your index finger are very close to the joint and might need to be taken out at some point, but we'll see how you go. For now, just take it easy. No more than a few minutes typing a day to begin with. If it hurts, stop. I'll see you every few days for the next couple of weeks and we can build up strength but in a controlled way."

Jodie looked at Brandon. He was grinning. She found her own smile forming.

"It's a miracle how well it's healing," Brandon said in wonder. "You can hardly see the scars."

Adam nodded. "The specialist she saw is one of the best." He looked at Jodie and smiled. "God has been very gracious to you."

———

JODIE WALKED beside Brandon back out to his truck. He stopped suddenly and took both her hands in his. He held them gently and smiled down at her. "I've wanted to do this for a long time,"

"Do what?"

"This." He held up her hands.

"Hold both of them at once?" She laughed. "I thought you were going to do something spectacular."

"Always." He grinned and tugged her closer. "I've also wanted to kiss you and feel both your hands hold me around my waist. Pure, naked skin, not a splint."

She blushed at the word naked. He laughed, tugging one of her arms and settling it on his back.

"Come on," he encouraged. "Squeeze me 'til I can't breathe."

She put her other arm around him and locked her hands together gently. Her right hand felt strange and ... yes, naked. Then she squeezed and he pretended to choke. She stepped back and swatted him.

He caught her hand in his. "This calls for celebration. We need to go somewhere you've never been before or do something you've never done before."

"Like what?"

He shrugged, then laughed. "To be honest, I have no idea. What about feeding a baby squirrel? Have you held a squirrel before?"

"No." A pair had built a nest in the tree outside her house once and she'd loved watching the babies. She'd forgotten about that. There were plenty of warm memories of Trinity Lakes. Many things she could show her children someday.

"You need to do it," he said, taking her hand and pulling her toward his truck.

"Where are we going? Where are these squirrels?"

"It's a secret." He opened the passenger door for her, smiled as she independently did up her seat belt, then went around to his side of the truck. "And you have to promise me you won't tell anyone. It could cause an uproar."

She frowned. What was he talking about? "Is your father looking after baby squirrels now?"

"Just Edward." He put his truck into gear and headed toward his father's place.

"Edward?"

"That's the squirrel's name."

"Why?" Jodie laughed. "How'd he come up with that name?"

Brandon shrugged and grinned over at her. "I don't know. You'll have to ask him."

Brandon led her into his dad's house, calling out to Edward as he went. A scratching noise came from the back room before a little squirrel bounded down the hall, scampered up Brandon's jeans and shirt to his shoulder. It perched there, making little chittering noises in his ear. Jodie's heart melted.

Brandon turned, lifted the squirrel from his shoulder and settled it in his hand. It perched there and scratched its nose.

"Edward, meet Jodie," Brandon said, holding the furry little creature out to her. "Jodie, my brother Edward. Adopted, of course."

Jodie laughed and hesitantly held out her hand. Edward

sniffed, clearly looking for food. His whiskers tickled her hand, his little nose cold and wet. Then his dark eyes blinked up at her.

"Aren't you gorgeous," she murmured, stroking his little ears.

"Look what you've done now, Eddie." Brandon lifted the squirrel and looked it in the eye. "Taken my girlfriend, just like that."

Jodie rolled her eyes. "You think I'm that fickle?"

He laughed and the sound warmed her heart. Being here with Brandon, hearing him speak affectionately to a squirrel, seeing the light in his eyes, she couldn't think of anywhere she'd rather be.

"Let's take him outside for a bit," Brandon said. "Dad worries about him being cooped up inside, but if he took him to work, it would soon get around that he's got a squirrel and you can imagine what Susannah would do with that."

Yes, she could imagine.

Brandon set Edward on his shoulder and took Jodie's hand. He led her out the back door. Jodie looked around. Was there room for a duck pond and state-of-the-art aviaries? She didn't think so.

Brandon settled on the garden seat and she sat beside him while Edward climbed along the back of the seat, making excited little barking noises.

"So what was that visit from Marla and Rhonda Ingalls about this morning?" Brandon leaned back against the seat.

She relayed their conversation and Brandon's eyes twinkled. "Sounds like Dad's got some unexpected allies." His gaze followed Edward's nimble steps along the fence and he looked thoughtful. "Might be worth considering."

"There needs to be a squirrel play park too." Jodie looked up at the maple they were sitting beneath. "What sort of trees do squirrels prefer?"

Brandon shrugged, looking amused. "No idea. You'd have to ask my dad."

They sat in silence for a while, enjoying the sunshine. She lifted her face to its warmth and smiled. She'd thought she'd be devastated she wasn't in New York, but she was feeling far from devastated. She was feeling content and at peace.

"Jodie?"

She turned to face him. "Yeah?" His expression was serious. She waited.

"Back in early high school, before Ariel, I had a few girl-friends."

She nodded. That didn't surprise her.

He pulled at a loose thread on the hem on his shirt. "None of them were serious, but I'm ashamed of the way I acted with them."

"In what way?"

"I was only out for myself. I liked them paying me attention but I was careless with their hearts. I dated them and dumped them when I got bored."

"So what was different about Ariel?"

He seemed to know what she was asking. What was it about Ariel that was so special? Why did he feel so rejected, so hurt when she turned him down?

He looked down, focusing on the loose thread. "She had something none of the others had. I didn't recognize it for what it was." His fingers stilled and he looked up and met her gaze. "She had the spirit of Jesus. She had true life. It shone from her even when she was sad or troubled. It drew me to her." He smiled and tugged on her hand, drawing it beneath his arm. "And you have that too."

Warmth filled her from head to toe. What greater compliment was there?

"So what about you?"

"You want to know about boyfriends?" The warmth dissipated. She bit her lip. "I had a crush on a guy named Hamish in my early teen years, but Rex Tyrangiel was my first boyfriend. We were living at the Bible college and we caught the school bus together."

"How old were you?"

"Five."

Brandon grinned. "That doesn't count."

"Why? Children are capable of great love." And loss. How well she knew that.

"Okay. Who was your last boyfriend?"

"He was."

"Really? So how long was he your boyfriend?"

"Two months."

Brandon sputtered into his sleeve, then hooted with laughter.

She pushed him. "What? That's a long time in a five-year old's life. It's like, what, two years in an adult's life."

"You're not very good at math, are you?" His look was affectionate as he drew her in for a side hug. He smiled down at her. "So what was the breakup over? He wouldn't share his toys?"

"He left. His parents finished their studies and left."

"Oh." There was a world of understanding in his eyes. Who'd have known Brandon Taylor was capable of such depth? Such empathy?

"It wasn't over the fact he sounded like a dinosaur?" he asked.

And then he went and ruined it. She blinked. What was he talking about?

"Rex Tyrangiel sounds very similar to Tyrannosaurus rex to me. Though I guess now you can say he's your Tyrannosaurus ex."

Jodie groaned, but she couldn't help laughing. "That is worse than any of Josh's jokes."

"Yeah, sorry." But he didn't look sorry.

Jodie took his hand and ran her finger along the tendons on his forearm. "I want us to honor God, Brandon. In our relationship. In everything."

Brandon's expression turned serious. "With God's help we can do it, Jodie. I truly believe that."

She smiled at him. "Me too."

CHAPTER TWENTY-THREE

Brandon pulled back into his dad's driveway after dropping Jodie home. Dad was collecting letters from the mailbox.

"How was work?" Brandon asked.

"Good." Dad opened the front door, chuckling when Edward scampered down the hall and climbed up his work clothes, sniffing all the way. "He hates that I smell like other creatures," Dad said with a smile. "He's about ready to go back into the wild."

"Jodie and I took him outside for a bit this afternoon."

Dad's mouth tipped. "Edward would've enjoyed that." His eyes said what his mouth didn't. Yes, Brandon had enjoyed it too.

Dad tore open an envelope bearing the council's logo and skimmed the letter. His expression darkened the more he read.

"More of the same," he said, with a disgusted grunt. "They pushed the new regulations through the council. You can only keep four fowl at a time on any suburban property. I have to move to the outskirts of town or have a bigger yard if I want any more."

Brandon frowned. "So our newspaper article didn't achieve

anything?" He looked around. Dad was caring for seven water-birds at the moment, including three geese, and sometimes he had more.

"Not with the council, anyway." Dad huffed and threw the letter on the table. "I'm not moving," he said, fire in his eyes. "This place belongs in our family. McAffrey's have been here for generations." He closed his eyes. "Even if I'm the last, I'm not going before I'm good and ready."

Hurt irritated Brandon's chest. He was a McAffrey too, wasn't he? Maybe not in name, but definitely by blood.

"Maybe I can continue the tradition."

Dad looked at him in silence, then sighed. "You have your own life. I wouldn't expect that of you. You've got a good job, your mother's house ..."

"That's now a hollow, empty shell."

Dad's eyes widened in surprise. "Well, you'd be more than welcome here, son. I just don't have room for you right now."

It was true. And Brandon knew better than to ask Dad to move into Mom's— his house.

"I could change my surname," Brandon said with a smile. "Make it McAffrey-Taylor so my children know their heritage."

Dad rolled his eyes. "Never had much liking for hyphenated names. Just people trying to sound important."

"Or people trying to honor both their parents."

"Yeah, or that." Dad rubbed his cheek, drawing Brandon's gaze again to the scar from the day Susannah had attacked him with her diamond ring. "So long as you've thought about your future kids," Dad said. "What name will they take on? It's a long name to have to learn to spell in kindergarten or to say every time they introduce themselves. Signatures and filling out forms would be a nightmare."

Dad had a good point.

"Maybe they can just go with McAffrey. It's a distinguished

name. And who knows? One of my kids might want to become a wildlife rehabilitator like you, rather than a mechanic."

"You wouldn't mind?" Dad turned his head to the side to allow the squirrel to climb down his shoulder.

"Not at all. I'd want my children to do what brings them life and joy."

Dad smiled and patted Brandon on the shoulder. "You're a good man."

———

BRANDON COULDN'T SLEEP. He paced the cold, empty house, his mind on his father's warm, cozy home. Dad needed somewhere for his animals. He looked around the house he and his mother had lived in for the past five years. It was a nice building, but it didn't mean anything to him. His memories of Mom here weren't memories he cared to hold onto. What if he were to sell? Could he then use the money to buy the cottage Josh lived in, next door to Dad's place? Josh had a fair-sized yard. They could pull down the fence and use both back yards to build the sheds and aviaries Marla and Rhonda dreamed of. Maybe something a bit less over the top, but something that would work.

First thing in the morning, he called Bob Ingalls.

"Is there any possibility the person who owns the cottage next door to Luke McAffrey would sell?"

"You mean the house Josh Ladan is renting?"

"That's the one."

"I doubt it would sell, what with all the drama over your dad's house. Why?"

Brandon sighed. He didn't want to tell Bob why. Bob would tell his wife, Marla, who would tell Rhonda who would tell the town.

"I'm interested in it because I'm thinking of selling my

mom's place —my place. It's too big, and I'd like to be next to my dad." Close enough to the truth.

"You'd be happy to kick your friend out?" Bob laughed, and the sound of it grated on Brandon's nerves.

"Maybe we'd share." And maybe not. Josh was going to be married in six months. He and Hallie would want to find a bigger place.

Bob hmphed. "Isn't there some kind of issue with your dad's place? Something to do with how many birds he's got there? I heard hundreds of dead mice were found there, and neighbors were complaining about the smell."

Anger heated Brandon's chest. "You believe that?"

"Whether I believe it or not, rumors like that will make it hard to sell."

Brandon's heart sank. "I'm telling you, it's not true."

"Okay." Bob didn't sound convinced.

"So do you think there's a possibility I could buy the place?" Brandon couldn't keep the irritation from his voice. "Should I try to find the owner and get in touch, or can you?"

"I will." Bob jumped in so quickly that Brandon smiled. He'd hit the right nerve. The last thing Bob wanted was to lose money on a potential sale.

"I'd appreciate it. Thanks, Bob."

Brandon ended the call and sighed. It shouldn't be so hard to get Bob to cooperate. The man had too much power in this town. Brandon was learning that power was dangerous when it was used to control or deceive.

In the meantime, he'd do his own research. Maybe find someone who was good with finances, someone who understood about buying and selling property. If only he had a relative in property

Lord? Who can I ask?

A name popped into his mind. Wayne Gilbertson. He laughed out loud.

Anyone else, Lord?

———

ON SUNDAY MORNING, Brandon awoke just in time to get ready for church. He raced into the bathroom to have a quick shower and shave, then opened his front blind. He stopped short. A familiar figure stood on his front porch.

"Dad?" He opened the door and his father turned with a sheepish smile, his intelligent green eyes crinkling in the corners.

"Thought maybe I could come to church with you instead of showing up by myself and feeling like a lone goose on a lake."

Brandon smiled and invited him in. "Don't you look handsome today?"

His dad looked down at his cotton shirt and tailored pants. "They're just clothes. Everyone wears them."

"Well, I hope so." Brandon grinned. "But I have to say, you look very much like me, so whatever clothes you're wearing, you're a handsome man."

His dad chuckled, a rich, full sound, and Brandon's heart warmed with affection. If he'd known what the Junk Man was really like, there was no way he would have ridiculed him for years. That was the problem with this town. People assumed things, believed what they heard instead of seeking out the truth for themselves. He knew because he'd been guilty of the same sin.

Lord, please let the truth be known.

"Can I get you a cup of coffee?" Brandon asked.

"Thank you. Edward woke one of my geese up early this morning so I'm about ready for another one."

Brandon chuckled as he started the coffee maker. "What did Edward do to the goose?"

"Who knows." Dad shook his head. "Cheeky little critter.

Maybe he's just decided he's ready to go back to the wild now summer's on its way."

Brandon brought two mugs of coffee to the table, placing the milk and sugar in front of his dad to let him make it the way he liked. He sat beside his father and they drank in silence for a few minutes before Dad put his cup down.

"Do you mind me coming to church with you?"

"Not at all." Brandon shook his head. "I never had a chance to go with Mom. She didn't believe in God until right at the end, when she was too sick to come."

"I'm sorry." Dad patted his shoulder.

"I used to envy the Ladans, coming in as a family each Sunday. I couldn't understand why Josh never wanted to sit with them."

Dad chuckled. "If you'd grown up coming to church with me or your mother, I imagine you wouldn't want to sit with me now either."

"Surely not." Brandon only half meant it.

"Don't worry. I won't embarrass you in church," Dad said with a grin.

"You think you know the etiquette?"

"Well, I grew up in the church," Dad said. Brandon nodded, remembering how surprised he'd been hearing Dad talk to Pastor Ladan like a seasoned Christian. "I just never took it to heart. But now it's as though all the truths are coming back, only this time I believe them."

Brandon knew what his father meant. He'd been the same. Had it not been for the accident with Jodie and his mother's passing, he may have continued on in the church, believing in his head but not living in his heart.

He couldn't be grateful for what had happened, but at the same time, he could see that God used it to bring about His perfect plan.

Dad took another sip of coffee and closed his eyes. He

almost always appeared calm and content, but surely sometimes a battle must rage inside at the injustice he'd experienced?

"Dad, do you ever resent me?" he asked before he could second-guess himself. "I mean, if it weren't for my mother, you'd still have your job as environmental planner and people would show you more respect. You might have found a wife, had a family."

Dad's brow furrowed and when he answered, his words were slow and thoughtful.

"Maybe I was angry with your mother for a time, but you weren't to blame. And if this hadn't happened, I probably wouldn't have had any time for God. I would have continued making as much money as I could, enjoying the prestige that came with my job, and playing the world's one-up game. I would never have valued justice so highly or been so concerned for God's creatures." His eyes met Brandon's. "And I have a family. You. I wouldn't change that for the world."

Brandon saw he meant it. He looked down at the tablecloth to hide his emotion. This morning he would walk into church beside his earthly father, knowing his Heavenly Father had blessed him more than he'd ever thought possible.

———

Brandon enjoyed walking into church beside his dad. To his surprise, Dad shook people's hands, nodded at them, and seemed to appreciate the connection. He was definitely not the shy hermit Brandon had once thought him to be.

Jodie slid into the seat beside them in the back row and Brandon reached for her hand. Rather than take it, she gave him a hug.

"Good to see you." She planted a kiss on his cheek.

His eyes widened. Now wouldn't that be a nice way to wake up every morning for the rest of his life? Woah. He needed to slow down, not get ahead of himself. Yet it was hard not to let hope build.

"I can go and sit somewhere else if you like," Dad said with a wink, nodding toward Jodie.

"No. Why would you do that?"

Dad grinned. "I don't know, give you some privacy?"

"To hold hands?" Brandon grinned back. "If it's not appropriate to do in front of my father, it's certainly not appropriate to do in church."

His dad chuckled and everyone fell quiet as the worship leader welcomed everyone to the service.

CHAPTER TWENTY-FOUR

Jodie smiled as she ate her breakfast. Adam had given her the all-clear to work and drive, and she felt free. First she'd see Selena and officially accept the position at the paper. Then she might drop in on Brandon at work and tell him the good news.

"Good morning." Mom pulled the milk out of the fridge and made herself a coffee. There were dark circles beneath her eyes, and her usual smile was absent.

Jodie set her spoon down in her bowl of cereal. "Are you alright, Mom?"

Mom looked up and set the milk on the counter. "I'm a bit worried about Esther. She needs our prayers."

"What's going on?"

"She's beginning to discover things about Mark she hadn't realized before."

"Like what?" Jodie's heart jarred. She'd only met Esther's boyfriend Mark once, so knew very little about him. Jodie had thought him good-looking but standoffish. She'd put his demeanor down to him being a school principal.

"He's decided to take a job in New York."

"And?"

"He decided without asking Esther."

"She doesn't have to go."

Mom bit her lip. "It seems Mark lodged a transfer on her behalf."

"Without telling her? Is that even legal?"

Mom sighed. "I don't know. He's the principal. But there's something strange going on." She took a sip of her coffee. "I'm beginning to think Esther doesn't come home because she's being manipulated. Pushed to isolate herself from family."

"You think he's abusing her?" Alarm filled her.

"Not physically."

"Emotionally?"

"Maybe." Mom's eyes glistened and Jodie felt guilty. She'd judged Esther. Given up on her. She should have fought harder to keep in contact. Should have refused to hang up when Esther said she was too busy to talk.

"If I'd gone to NYU ..."

"You'd be in New York and could reconnect with her. Make sure she was alright." Mom nodded. "I know. I thought of that too. But God has closed that door for now. It's okay. God has our Essie. He's with her even when we can't be."

Jodie swallowed hard, no longer hungry. She'd told herself she didn't need her sister in her life, but the truth was, she missed Esther. Missed her so much it hurt. And the thought that Mark wasn't treating her right ... A memory stirred of a phone call last year. After several attempts, she'd finally managed to speak to Esther. They'd been talking, but Esther had cut her off. Said Mark had arrived. Esther never talked to her while Mark was around. Did Mark not allow her to talk to her family? No, it didn't make sense. Esther was strong. She was the brightest, bubbliest person Jodie knew.

Lord, protect and keep her please. Give her wisdom.

Selena was thrilled to see Jodie.

"I've got your paperwork ready," she said. "Come to the computer, and I'll show you the work and study schedule I've put together. We can adjust it as we need to."

She nudged Jodie into a chair in front of the desk that would be hers and turned on the computer. Jodie smiled at her enthusiasm.

"And here's some applications for online courses that looked good. They all have flexible part-time options that would work perfectly for your internship here."

Jodie flipped through the forms, pausing at the familiar name and logo on one of them. NYU. Ironic that NYU was where she'd be if not for her injured hand. She began filling out a form and tried to put New York from her mind. And Esther. Because thinking about Esther scared her. She'd thought her sister was so happy. How could a relationship turn like that? It was unsettling.

"I'll leave you to it," Selena said, then paused and looked back. "I'm so pleased you've said yes, Jodie. You have a gift. You have a way with words, and you understand people."

Oh, no she didn't. She'd allowed her insecurities to rule for years. She'd believed Esther had abandoned her, like everyone else who'd left Trinity Lakes. But Esther was her sister. Jodie shouldn't have given up on her so easily. Should have realized something more was going on.

She tried to focus on what she was doing. Reapplying to NYU, this time for a part-time course, was bittersweet.

"Brandon, another one of your girlfriends is here to see you," Bruce called through the roller door.

Brandon frowned. Not helpful, Bruce. He couldn't help it that Rachel Kearn had flirted with him when she brought her car in this morning. Once he would have shut her down with one biting comment, but he was learning to be gentle. Learning not to judge. And Rachel was a sister in Christ. So he'd mentioned Jodie as often as he could and hoped that would work.

He smiled when he saw Jodie, but she didn't smile back. Had she heard Bruce's comment?

He drew her into his arms. "What's wrong?"

"I told Selena I'll work for her. I thought that's what God wanted me to do, but ..."

Brandon's heart sank. "But what?"

She lifted her head, her worried eyes meeting his. "Esther's going to New York because her boyfriend put in a transfer for her ... without asking her. Mom thinks there's something not right between her and Mark. If I was there ..."

"You think you could fix it?"

"Yes. No. I don't know. I could be there for her."

Brandon hurt to see the pain in her eyes. He wanted Jodie here with him, he really did, but he also wanted what was best for her.

She pulled back from his hug, her brow furrowed. "What was Bruce saying about girlfriends?"

So she'd heard. He rolled his eyes. "Being smart. Rachel came in with her car and was being very friendly. Don't worry—I talked about you every chance I got." He touched a finger to her nose. "I think she got the picture."

Her eyes widened and she grabbed his hand. "Brandon. Is there a grease mark there now?"

"Could be." He grinned, glad he'd distracted her from her worries.

She wiped at her nose with the bottom of her shirt, and he

laughed. Surely grease on her shirt was worse than having it on her skin.

He drew her back into his arms. "There's nothing there."

Jodie pushed him back toward the workshop. "You'd better not spend all your time flirting with girls."

He laughed. "Just one," he said, but headed back to work. "I'll be praying for Esther."

"Thanks." She walked away.

———

JODIE PULLED a coffee cup from the cupboard and absently glanced at her phone. A new email had come in.

NYU?

She put the cup on the counter and frowned as she read it, then re-read it. Was this a joke? It had to be some kind of scam. Her heart fluttered too fast in her chest, confusion swirling.

"I don't understand," she whispered.

Mom looked over her shoulder. "What is it?"

Jodie held out her phone. "It looks like an offer of place at NYU, all fees covered."

Mom frowned. "I thought they said they couldn't renew your scholarship."

"They did. This is an internship offer based on the article I wrote for the Trinity Lakes Gazette."

"Did you send it in?"

"No."

"Did Selena?"

"She must've put it in with my application for online study." Jodie bit her lip. Excitement warred with confusion. She couldn't leave Selena now, could she? Especially when Selena was the one who'd submitted the article on her behalf.

Mom read the email in silence, then handed back Jodie's

phone, eyes shining with pride. "Exceptional talent," she said, repeating the words of the email. "I'm so proud of you."

Jodie managed a wobbly smile. "Mom, what do I do?"

"Pray about it. Wait for God's direction."

Easy to say. She had a week to respond to the offer. Her thoughts and emotions were tangled. It had seemed so clear God was directing her to the position with Selena but then this … And what about Esther? Did she need her help in New York?

How was she supposed to know what God wanted? Was He giving her a choice? Testing her?

She didn't want to give up Brandon, but maybe God was asking her to. To give her life to Him alone, heart, soul, mind, and strength. Because the strength of her feelings for Brandon couldn't be good, could they? What if she became like Esther and became so caught up with Brandon that she couldn't think for herself?

New York had been her dream for years. A dream she'd thought had been crushed.

Slowly, she went up to her room, pulled out her old journals. and began to read. How had she forgotten her dream of New York so easily? She couldn't base her life choices around someone else. She couldn't stay here just because Brandon was here. He could break up with her at any moment. It wasn't like they were engaged or married. And there was no way Brandon would go to New York for her. His apprenticeship contract required him to work at Trinity Lakes Auto for at least another two years. His life was here. His job. His family.

———

JODIE'S SLEEP was restless that night. Filled with vivid dreams of Hamish leaving, of Esther holding off Mark while he came at her with a knife, of Brandon kissing Rachel, all scenes so real she struggled to separate dreams from reality when she woke.

Her grief was real, relived, and now experienced anew. She knew what she needed to do.

————

Jodie had texted to say they needed to talk. Urgently. Brandon quickly changed after work and headed down to the lake.

He saw Jodie immediately. She sat on a bench, looking out over the lake, her blonde ponytail blowing in the wind. He smiled. He'd never thought he could love someone so deeply. Be so … connected.

She looked up and accepted his hug. He took her hand but she pulled hers away.

"Brandon, I've been offered an internship in New York."

"Okay?" He had to remain calm. He needed to consider Jodie and her dreams, not selfishly cling to his own. "I thought you'd already committed to working with Selena."

"I haven't officially started yet."

He forced a smile. "I guess this is exciting, isn't it?"

"It is, but … what about us?" She avoided his gaze.

He shrugged. "This doesn't change anything. I'll miss you, of course, but we can have a long-distance relationship."

"It's not that simple, Brandon. This changes everything."

It did? A clamp tightened around his heart.

She looked down at her feet. "A long-distance relationship wouldn't work."

"Why not?" He wished he could see what she was thinking, what was going on here. It didn't make sense.

She bit her lip. "You might think it will, but I know better. People promise to write, to keep in touch, and they mean it at the time, but they never do. It's out of sight, out of mind."

Poor Jodie. She'd been so hurt by those who had left in the past. "Not for me. I'd think of you every moment of every day."

She shook her head. "You say that now. What about when a

pretty girl like Rachel comes along? When she's right here in front of you, interested in you?"

He laughed. "I'd tell her all about how much I love you." He reached for her hand but she pulled it away. His smile faded. "Jodie, I will remain faithful."

"You think you will, but—"

"You don't trust me to keep my word? You think I'm like everybody else who's abandoned you?"

"This isn't about whether or not I trust you. It's about what I know. What experience has taught me." She crossed her arms defensively.

Wow. Why was she acting like the old Jodie, shutting him out? He tried to remain patient, calm, despite his heart hammering in his chest. "There's absolutely no reason we can't manage a long-distance relationship with the way technology is now. We can talk to each other and even see each other every day. I won't forget you."

She made a frustrated noise. "I'll already be looking at screens all day for work and for study."

It was an irrational excuse. He shook his head, desperation clawing deep within. Maybe she'd had enough of him. Maybe she didn't feel for him the way he felt about her. And yet her eyes, her actions, had said otherwise. Until now.

"I'm going to be gone four years or more," she said.

"You'll be home for holidays." Or not. Esther rarely came home. It was a sore point with the family. He'd seen their confusion, their longing to see her. Surely Jodie wouldn't do the same? Was this about him or about her?

He touched her arm. "Jodie, in two years I'll be free of my obligations with Trinity Auto. I could find a job in New York."

"Brandon, don't say things you don't mean."

"I do mean it."

"It wouldn't be fair on your dad. You're the only family he

has." She looked out at the lake, avoiding his eyes. "I'm just glad God didn't let our hearts get too involved."

Too involved? His heart was already there. It was being crushed harder with every word she spoke.

She met his eyes then. "I mean, I'm grateful for this time with you. God kept me here for this. To be able to comfort you in the loss of your mother. To be there for you as you met with Ariel's family. To be there as you grew closer to your dad and realized you have family in him and in God."

What about so he could be there for her, too? Why was she making this all about her giving to him? Hadn't she received too? He'd thought they had a two-way relationship. Giving to one another. Loving one another. A lump filled his throat.

"Jodie, don't do this. Please." His voice came out hoarse.

"Don't, Brandon." She stood. "I need to go home. I've got a lot of thinking and planning to do."

"And praying," he said, but she didn't acknowledge she'd heard.

"Lord?" Brandon didn't know what else to pray. He walked around his house feeling lost, the most alone he'd felt since Mom died. "Where are you in this, Lord? Please show me."

He loved Jodie Ladan, and now he'd tasted what it could be like to be so much more than her friend, mere friendship would never be enough. But he didn't deserve her. He'd always known that. Always feared she'd realize it and walk away. He'd thought things were special between them. That this would last. What a fool he'd been. She'd given him so much. Well, this was what he needed to give to her. The freedom to leave him behind. Completely.

"Oh, Lord." His heart squeezed painfully. "Show me what to do. Help me through this, please."

He rested his head against the window and looked out at the beautiful summer day. The sky was a bright blue. He wanted to share it with Jodie. Wanted to experience every season with her. But he couldn't pressure her to stay. Wouldn't do it.

"Lord, am I not enough? Is that why she's leaving? Is that why she's cutting me off?"

She's afraid. She's leaving you so you don't leave her first.

He knew the thoughts came from somewhere deeper than his own mind and heart. He looked up at the sky. "Lord? How do I help her not be afraid?

She'd told him how everyone had left. Rex Tyrangiel was more than a cute story. He'd been her first love. He'd broken her little-girl heart when he'd left.

But what could he do about it?

Pray.

He moved to the kitchen table and sat down. He missed Mom. He missed her so much it was a physical ache in his chest. But knowing Jodie was leaving was worse. His mother loved him, would have chosen to stay. But Jodie was choosing to leave. Not just physically, but emotionally as well.

CHAPTER TWENTY-FIVE

D ad listened to Brandon, eyes full of sympathy.

"I've been praying for her, but I can't force her to do anything," Brandon said, fighting the lump in his throat. "I have to let her go."

"Really?" Dad sat across from him at the table, an injured goose in his lap. He wound a bandage around the splint on its leg.

"You think there's another option?"

Dad didn't speak for a minute. He concentrated on the goose, tucking its wings under his elbow with practiced ease as he worked. Then he looked up.

"What would have happened if I'd gone after your mother? I loved her. What if I'd found her, challenged her thinking about why she was running away, and worked it out with her?"

He'd never thought of that. "I don't know. What do you think would've happened?"

"I don't know." Dad's mouth tipped. "Maybe she would have come back, maybe she wouldn't. But one thing I do know is I wouldn't have all the what-ifs racing around my heart and mind. I wouldn't have been wondering all those years what I could have done differently and if it would have made a difference. She would have known how I felt about her. I could have given her that much."

Given her that much. Dad's words swirled around his heart and mind. Jodie had implied she'd been the one giving all this time. He knew it wasn't true, but maybe he needed to make it clear he was giving too. He would speak God's truth to her the way she had so often to him in the past. But he would do it in love. He would make sure she knew how he felt about her. He would give to her with no expectation of anything in return. The way Jesus did for him.

———

BRANDON KNOCKED on the doorframe of Jodie's room. His heart sank at the sight of all the boxes spread across the floor. She looked up from where she stood by her desk. Froze. The dismay that came over her face did nothing to help his heart.

"What are you doing here?" Her tone was accusatory.

"I wanted to see how you're doing."

"Why?"

He sighed and sat down on her swivel chair. "Because that's what friends do."

Her hands went to her hips. "You're happy being friends? Is that what you're saying?"

He saw her defensiveness for what it was. A barrier. A protective wall around her heart that had pushed him out.

"I think we're a little bit more than friends, Jodie." He sighed. "Look, I get that you're scared, but I'm worried you're going to make the choice to leave out of fear rather than hearing what God wants for you."

"What makes you think I'm scared?"

"The way you're shutting me out again. It's like you've gone back to your default of avoiding the pain of people leaving. If you cut me off, you hold the power. This is about you not being able to trust me. Or God."

She came closer, eyes full of fire and shook a finger in his face. "You think you know so much about me, don't you? This is what you've always been like. Watch everybody, try to find out their secrets, judge their weaknesses so you can throw them back in their face when the time is right."

"Jodie." He said her name quietly, but she'd spun back around and was throwing books into a box. She dropped one and he saw what it was. Koala Lou.

Relief filled his soul. She'd packed that one months ago, which meant she had unpacked again. She hadn't always been planning to leave. She'd changed her mind about her dreams at some point. Had stopped fighting for NYU. And that renewed his hope.

"Jodie?" he said her name again and she dropped the book. She bent to pick it up, dropped it again. It was like déjà vu. She tried for another book instead. It looked like her Bible. But her injured hand couldn't hold it. With a cry she let it go, watching it fall open on the carpet, years' worth of Sunday bulletins and notes falling out and floating across the floor.

She sank to her knees, scrambling to pick them up.

Brandon came to her side, squatted beside her, and they gathered them together. He righted her Bible, tucked them in the front, and held it out to her, but she didn't reach for it. She didn't look at him, but he saw the tears that began slipping down her cheeks, one by one. His heart broke for her.

JODIE WANTED TO RUN. She needed to escape. She couldn't even hold her Bible. Her hand that had supposedly healed wouldn't let her pack.

She felt Brandon's eyes on her but couldn't look up. She was confused. Years of hurt over lost friendships spilled from her soul and down her cheeks. No one ever remembered her once they left. And when she left, she couldn't trust anyone to remember her. Not even Brandon.

"Jodie," Brandon said as he stood and pulled her to her feet. "Please don't do this."

She rubbed her wet eyes, still unable to look at him. She knew the moment she met his green eyes she would be captivated again, unable to deny the depth of her feelings.

"Do what?"

"Shut me out."

"What makes you think I'm shutting you out? I'm just busy packing. You know that New York has been my dream for years. It's not personal."

"Really?"

She moved to another box and threw some clothes in. She'd planned to pack them in a suitcase, but this gave her something to do. The last thing she wanted Brandon to do was help her get her suitcase down from the top of her closet because her hands couldn't hold it steady. One shirt went in. Another. Another.

"Jodie, please look at me."

"Why? You think that every girl who looks at you is smitten? You think you can play your games with me? Beguile me with your handsome half-smile and brilliant green eyes?"

"No." He touched her arm. Just gently, but it was as though a jolt of electricity went through her, followed by warmth and a tingling she couldn't deny. Why did he do this to her? What was wrong with her?

"I get that you're scared," he said. "I'm scared, too. Love isn't simple. It's hard. But it looks out for the best in the other person. It lets them go if they truly want to go, but it also speaks the truth when they are in denial. Jodie, I'm speaking the truth in love. If you leave now and cut me off out of fear, you'll always regret it." He ran his hands down his face. "And so will I."

She heard the sadness in his voice, like a living presence in the room. Unable to help herself, she turned to look at him. Met his eyes and saw grief mixed with compassion. For her.

"Are you ending our relationship because God wants you to?" he asked, "If you know He's asked you to, you go with my blessing. But I suspect there's more to it."

There was no pride in his words, no mockery, no manipulation. Just pure truth. And love.

She remembered the day he'd rescued her from the spider. He hadn't held it over her. He hadn't even mentioned it again. He respected her vulnerabilities, wanted to help meet her needs, wanted her to let him love her.

He came closer, tugged at her arm, drew her in.

Oh Jesus, help me. I'm so tired of fighting. So tired ...

With a sob, she fell against his chest. His arms came around her. He moved her back to the chair and pulled her onto his lap. He cradled her against his chest, stroking her hair and pressing featherlight kisses on the top of her head.

"You're right," she whispered through tears. "I'm scared."

"Me too, Jodie. Me too." His arms tightened.

"I don't know what to do." She looked up, her chin trembling. "I want to trust you. I do."

"Then trust God. Trust that He's in me, His Spirit working, growing me, making me into the man I'm supposed to be. A man you can trust." He looked down at her shaking hands. Still weak, but now trembling from emotion rather than fatigue.

He took her hand in one of his, then reached into his pocket with the other. "I have something I want to give you. It's not to pressure you into anything, not to make you feel you have to decide your future one way or another." He drew something out. "I want you to have this."

Jodie managed to pull her eyes away from his to look at the bracelet he held in his hand. It sparkled in the light, looking odd in his work-roughened hands.

"It was your mother's." She reached for it, swallowing hard. "I saw her wearing it."

He nodded, watching her study it. "I want to marry a girl like you some day, Jodie. I want to be able to give, to look out for her, to put her needs above my own."

Her eyes darted to his. "A girl like me?" Exactly what Hamish had said before his letters had stopped coming.

"Not a girl. Just you." He swallowed hard and his distinctive green eyes captured hers. "Only you."

He lifted her wrist, his fingers grazing her skin as he clasped the bracelet.

"No matter what, Jodie, I won't ever forget you. I'll think about you every single day of my life."

He really meant it. She couldn't answer, couldn't speak. Cradled here in his arms she felt safe, treasured, valued. Why was she fighting against him? Why was she fighting against depending on each other, depending on God?

"I know I'm not worthy of you," Brandon said, his face close to hers, "but I hope that wherever God leads you you'll always remember you are loved. By God and by me. You're a treasure, Jodie-Lee Ladan. I've never met anyone else like you, and I know I never will." He bent and gently brushed his lips against hers. It was a goodbye. He was letting her go.

"Brandon, wait." Longing warred with fear. She couldn't let him go. Not without speaking the truth. She put her hands either side of his face, fire lighting within. "You are worthy. God says you are worthy."

"I know." Still, his eyes were hauntingly sad. "But I also understand you leaving me behind, Jodie, I truly do. I am worthy in God's eyes, but all I have to offer anyone is a life in small-town Trinity Lakes with a mediocre job and a father the town is trying to kick out. You deserve more than that."

"No. That's not true. Susannah is the only one trying to kick Luke out. And this town is beautiful. Your job, it's a stable, respectable job helping people. And you…" Her lips hovered over his. "You are irresistible."

There were no other words to describe him. He'd laid his heart at her feet. Freely given, no strings attached. She touched her lips to his. Felt the desperation and longing in his kisses as he clung to her. His passion fueled her own and overwhelming love and desire filled her. She wanted him. There was no denying it. She could try to push him away all she liked, but Brandon Taylor would always own her heart.

He pulled back and pushed her gently off his lap before standing and taking a step back. "Jodie, we can't … I'm not trying to manipulate you."

She licked her lips, still tingling from the heat of his kisses. "I know."

He walked to the door of her room, then looked back. "Demo day, Jodie. We need to demolish any lies of the enemy. Use the weapons God has given you. Truth and love. I know He'll show you His plan for you. Not my plans. Not your plans. His good and perfect plan. I'll be praying you hear His voice. Only His."

With that, he was gone, the echo of his footsteps on the stairs leaving her heart bereft.

CHAPTER TWENTY-SIX

J odie jogged downstairs, carrying her wastepaper basket. She needed to empty the used tissues into the trash can. How could one person cry so many tears?

Mom and Dad were talking in the living room. Everything in her wanted to join them. She needed them right now, craved their loving care, but pride held her back. Rarely did she ask their opinion on anything. Josh and Esther were the ones who'd needed help and advice over the years. She'd never wanted to be the typical youngest child, always in trouble, always reckless, always needing help. She didn't want to be the stay-at-home child, clingy and needy, always sponging off her parents.

Despite her quiet steps, Dad looked up as she walked past the door. "Jodie." He smiled, his eyes crinkling in the corners, delight shining from them. "How are you doing?"

She put down her bin and tried to hold back more tears. She had to tell the truth. "Not good. I can't hear God anymore. I can't hear his voice." Her voice shook.

Mom patted the couch. "Join us?"

Jodie came into the room and sat beside Mom, wiping at red

and weepy eyes. Dad moved to sit directly across from them, his observant gaze missing nothing.

Mom took her hand, studied the scars.

"It's so weak," Jodie said. "I was trying to pack, but it's so weak."

"It'll take time, but it will heal." Mom's eyes met hers, looking somewhere deep inside. "Sometimes the heart takes longer."

Jodie blinked as tears burned the back of her eyelids. Mom clearly heard the words she didn't say. She drew in a deep breath.

"Mom, what do you and Dad think I should do about New York?"

"What do we think?" Mom sat back and looked at Dad. She saw the silent message that passed between them.

He rubbed a hand down his beard. "We think we'll miss you if you go, but we also think you're old enough and wise enough to listen to God and make the right decision."

"Do you think going is the right decision?"

Again, that look between her parents. Then Dad clasped his hands together in front of him and leaned forward, looking out the window, his brow furrowed.

"You don't, do you?" She could see it in his eyes, the struggle he was having to express his thoughts.

Mom cleared her throat, then looked at her, eyes filled with compassion. "Jodie, it's hard for us to hear God clearly on this, because we never want to let you go. Everything in us wants to keep you under our roof, in our home, safe, forever."

"Because I'm the youngest, most needy?"

"What?" Dad sat up, eyes wide. "No. No, you're our independent one. Too much so, really. Sometimes we've wished you needed us more. Not because we want you to struggle, but because it gives us a way to show we love you as deeply as we love Josh and Esther. When Josh had his accident and all our attention was on him for months, you were so strong, so mature. You understood our need to focus on him. And when Esther moved away, you wished her all the best and sent her with your blessing even though we knew your heart must've been breaking. We wanted to comfort you. To be there for you. To be needed."

She bit her lip and tears filled her eyes as she looked between her parents. "I need you now." All those years she'd fought to be worthy of this family, to be strong and independent, when God had given her this family as a gift. Why hadn't she been able to accept what He'd given?

"We're here." Dad's words were quiet and deep. In them, she felt the love of God. God, who was also here for her. Who didn't expect her to be perfect. Who didn't expect her to be extraordinary because she was a Ladan. Who loved her just the way she was. Who wanted to help her and provide others to love and help her.

"I'm confused about so many things." She couldn't continue. A tear ran down her cheek.

Mom moved closer and wrapped her arms around her, holding her close, letting her cry.

"We have the God who brings light and understanding to our chaos and confusion," Dad said. "James says if we ask for wisdom, God will give it."

Jodie remembered Dad's recent sermon on the book of James. It was so simple. All she had to do was be willing to admit she had a need. Be willing to ask.

God, I need your wisdom. Please.

She drew in a shuddery breath. "The truth is, deep down, I don't want to go."

Dad didn't even blink. Just continued watching her, that open, caring expression on his face.

"I liked the idea of it. The idea of being independent, of doing something special and extraordinary, of being the one who chose to leave. It made me feel ... powerful. In control."

"Why do you think you feel the need to be in control?"

Because I'm afraid. It was so clear now.

"Because I have trouble trusting God with my future. I have trouble trusting He will bring me through any pain or loss that comes my way. I have trouble trusting Him with my feelings and love for other people."

"Like Brandon?" She heard the smile in Mom's voice.

"Like Brandon." She ran her finger along the scar on her hand. "And if I stayed, I'd be such a hypocrite. I was forever making fun of Josh for living at home in his twenties, for not making his own way in life."

"Sounds like pride issues to me," Dad said, but he was smiling.

"I thought I'd worked through all that after my accident." She turned to Mom. "But when you said Esther's moving to New York ..."

"Esther isn't your responsibility." Mom pushed a strand of hair back from Jodie's face. "And it's not certain yet that she's going."

"It's not?"

"No. Everything's still up in the air."

Dad rubbed his beard. "Do you want to know my thoughts about all this?"

"Please."

"God provided you with a job right here, right now, doing what God has called you to do. Most people have to do years of study before they're offered a job like that. God also provided you with a very special young man who loves you deeply. Right here."

"So you wouldn't mind if I stayed home longer? You wouldn't lose respect for me?"

"Oh, Jodie," Dad came across and squished onto the couch beside her so that she was cushioned between him and Mom. He drew her into his arms. "We couldn't be more proud of you.

Only a strong young woman can put aside years of assumptions and pride and admit she's been wrong. To accept help. To accept love."

She leaned against his chest, hearing the steady beat of his heart against her ear. Feeling Mom's arm around her from the other side. She hadn't accepted a hug from her parents in a long, long time. Esther and Josh were the affectionate ones. She'd never allowed herself to be.

"We love you, Jodie-Lee," Mom said into her hair. "From the moment we knew we were finally expecting again, we loved you."

"Finally?"

Dad nodded. "We always wanted three children. And deep in my heart I hoped for another little girl. Just like you."

"And you've lived up to your name in every way," Mom said. "God increased our family and increased our joy by giving you to us. You have added so much to our lives. God be praised."

"Lived up to my name?" Jodie pulled back, a vague memory stirring.

"Jodie is Jewish, derived from Joseph. It means Jehovah shall add."

"And Lee?" It came out breathless.

"It means shelter. A sheltered place. You are sheltered under the wings of the almighty. He held you. He holds you. He'll never let go. And He is the one who gives us good things. He adds to our lives. You've lost friends, but He's given you new friends. Special friends like Brandon."

Something heavy, like a tombstone, rolled away from her heart, and light and warmth filled the place. "Oh, Mom. Dad." She squeezed them tight. "I love you. God knew I needed you. He knew exactly what He was doing when He placed me in this family."

Dad smiled. "I expect he has another family for you too

someday. Why don't you go and see Brandon? Put him out of his misery. Tell him exactly what's on your heart."

She would do exactly that. In truth and love. She left the living room with a bounce in her step, wishing she'd poured her heart out to Mom and Dad a long time ago.

———

BRANDON RUBBED his eyes with the back of his hand. He'd probably smeared grease across his face but he didn't care. He'd been praying for Jodie constantly. He was back at work, but his heart and mind were elsewhere. The long weekend hadn't been the break he'd hoped for.

Ryder, the new apprentice, loped into the workshop. "A man out there wants to see you."

"Oh?" Brandon wiped his hands on a rag and looked out the roller door. Bob Ingalls stood out the front, talking into his phone. He finished the call as Brandon approached, putting the phone back in his pocket.

"Brandon. You want the good news or the bad news first?"

Surely he didn't expect an answer to that? It seemed he did. "Good, I suppose."

Bob beamed. "The owner is keen to sell. He's been looking at selling because of—well, because."

Brandon stifled his smile. Because of his dad's geese. "And?"

"The bad news?"

Yes. Brandon refused to ask for it again. Whatever little power game Bob was playing, he was sick of it. Bob seemed to realize.

"The bad news is his lawyer has been threatening the council with a lawsuit. Susannah Gilbertson is an old contact of his and may have given him an exaggerated version of the condition of your dad's house."

Brandon clenched his fists. He'd wondered why the council was listening to Susannah. Now he knew.

"Do you think he'd drop the lawsuit if I offered a reasonable price for the house?"

"I don't think it would make any difference. The council has passed the regulations now. And the owner insists he wants full price for the house … and a bit more."

Brandon frowned. He hadn't found anyone to talk to and get advice from yet. "How much?"

Bob named the price, then grinned. "The good news again, though—you'd get that and more if you sold your mother's … I mean, your house."

Brandon's mind worked fast. The cottage beside Dad's was worth way more to him than his mother's house. It had a great sized yard, big enough for the council to stop harassing Dad about his animals. If he wanted to extend the cottage or even demolish and rebuild it someday, there was enough room for that too.

The problem was, Bob could be taking him for a complete ride. He really did need to find someone to ask advice.

God?

Wayne Gilbertson. Maybe the idea wasn't so ludicrous after all.

He looked at Bob. "I'll be in touch."

"Well, it needs to be soon." Bob didn't look pleased. "I've gone out of my way to get in touch with the owner for you."

Brandon nodded. "I appreciate that, but I'll go out of my way to make sure I'm a good steward of the finances God gives me."

Bob blinked fast, then gave Brandon and abrupt handshake before taking his leave.

So many things so up in the air. His future. Jodie's future. His relationship with her.

Lord? I leave her in your hands. I trust you.

And he meant it.

His heart was prayerful as he went back to work on the car.

"Brandon? Another visitor for you." Startled, Brandon pulled back from under the hood of the car.

"Sorry," Ryder said. "I just thought you'd want to see her."

Her?

———

Jodie followed Brandon's every move as he strode toward the front of the workshop, wiping his hands on a rag. His thick dark hair was mussed and a streak of grease smeared his cheek beneath his eye. She smiled. He'd never looked so good. He walked tall with confidence, every move reflecting his strength of body and character.

He looked up. Met her gaze and stopped walking. "Jodie."

She held up the tub in her hands. "I brought something for you."

The uncertainty in his troubled expression pulled at her heart. She'd done that to him. He took a few cautious steps forward and came to stop directly in front of her. He took the tub from her outstretched hands, his look questioning.

"Honest to Goodness All-Natural Hand Cleanser," he read out loud. "Perfect for removing stains from hands that know hard work."

"Leah got it as a special order through her organics store for me." Was he pleased? She couldn't tell.

"Really?" He looked surprised, the troubled pleat of his brow easing. "When did you order this?"

"Weeks ago."

A smile tilted his lips and she breathed easier.

"Do you like the brand name?"

He ran a grease-covered finger across the words. "Honest to Goodness. It's perfect." His eyes moved to her wrist. "You're wearing my mom's bracelet."

"Yeah." She drew in a tremulous breath. "I don't need to really. I mean, I plan to be with you in person at least once every single day of my life, so I don't need the reminder, do I?"

"Jodie?" He whispered her name, his eyes searching hers.

She smiled. "I'm staying, Brandon. No more fear. No more lies. Just honest-to-goodness truth. I love Trinity Lakes. I love the idea of working with Selena. My parents love me and want me to stay. And I love you."

His mouth opened and closed and his eyes searched hers. "That's a whole lot of love," he finally said.

"Yeah." There was so much she wanted to say. So much in her heart she wanted to share, but all she could do was stand there, captivated by the hope shining in his eyes, captivated by him.

"You're really staying?" he whispered. "You want to be with me?"

She nodded. "I don't want to run. I don't want to live in fear, I don't want to try to control a love that's uncontrollable, a gift from God. I love you Brandon. You are my dream, the dream God's given me."

"I so want to hug you right now, but—" He looked down at his filthy work clothes.

"I don't care about a bit of dirt." She came closer, gently took the tub of cleanser from his hands and placed it on the ground. Then she touched the smear of grease on his cheek. Traced it all the way down until her finger touched his lips. He drew in a shuddery breath, watching her every move. He was waiting for her, she realized. He needed to know this was what she wanted. Her eyes never leaving his, she placed both arms around his neck and pulled his head down until her lips touched his. At first he didn't move a muscle, but as her kiss deepened she felt his lips move beneath hers, warm and compliant. She was vaguely aware of Ryder whistling and making some kind of remark in the background, but she didn't care. Let the world know she loved Brandon Taylor.

She pulled back just far enough to see his eyes. Green and alive.

"I love you, Brandon. Honest to goodness love that I can't deny. For years I asked God to help me conquer my feelings for you, but I can't fight them anymore. The truth is, there is a time to love. And that time is now."

A laugh bubbled up in Brandon's throat. Then he lifted her and swung her around, laughing with abandonment and joy.

She held onto him, arms locked around his neck. She didn't intend to ever let him go.

CHAPTER TWENTY-SEVEN

Brandon took Jodie with him to see Josh later that evening. Hallie opened the door, and Brandon wondered again what would happen if he bought this cottage with its spacious yard. Had Josh and Hallie planned to live there after they were married?

"Please, come in," Hallie invited, stepping aside. Brandon hid his amusement. Hallie was always so proper. The opposite of Josh. But that's what made them good for each other.

"Hey guys," Josh said with a welcoming grin. "I hid the cookies so don't even try to find them."

Brandon chuckled. If that wasn't a challenge, he didn't know what was. To his surprise, Jodie didn't charge toward the kitchen. Instead, her fingers wrapped around his. He glanced at her and saw the promise in her eyes. She was here for him, whatever he had to say. He hadn't even told his father yet. Nerves skittered in his stomach.

Lord, please give me the words.

"Have a seat." Hallie pointed to the living room. Brandon sat, and to his surprise, Jodie sat on his lap.

Hallie giggled. "I guess this means you're not going to New York?"

Jodie grinned in reply and put her arms around his neck, holding him tighter. He swallowed. She was being very distracting right now.

"What do you mean?" Josh demanded. "I thought we knew she wasn't going."

Hallie rolled her eyes. "Josh, where have you been? There's been so much drama around here lately I can't believe you missed it."

"What? I've been right here. You didn't tell me anything."

"Because it was right in front of your eyes. Jodie got offered an internship in New York. She was even packing to go."

"What? No."

Brandon laughed. He couldn't help it. He'd always been the more observant of the two, but clearly Josh was completely oblivious to what had been going on around him.

"It doesn't matter," Brandon said, planting a kiss on Jodie's cheek. "She's staying now. The real reason I'm here is about the cottage."

"The cottage?" Josh's bewildered expression was laughable. "This one? What have I missed?"

"Don't worry, sweetheart, it didn't burn down while you weren't looking," Hallie said with a fond smile.

"Huh?"

Jodie giggled and soon Hallie was giggling too. Brandon bit back a laugh. The way this was going he'd never get out what he needed to say.

"Guys. I'm thinking of buying this place from your landlord. My dad needs more room for his creatures with this new regulation the council's put in place. Your back yard will be perfect. I thought maybe I can live here with Josh until you two get married and find a place of your own. Or if you two want to live here after you're married, I'll move in with Dad—so long as we can still use the backyard. You two like squirrels, don't you? And geese?"

Everyone was staring at him.

"Picture a playground out the back, Mark Rober style." He moved his arm. "A climbing frame here." He pointed to the other side of the room. "A swinging rope there, a ladder up into a little squirrel house in the middle."

"Wait!" Hallie held up her hand. "What are you talking about? And who is Mark whoever?"

"Mark Rober," Josh said, putting an arm around her. "He's an engineer and YouTuber who made an amazing obstacle course for his squirrels."

"A ninja warrior course," Brandon said. "And he named all the squirrels. There's Phat Gus, Marty—"

"And you want to put one in our backyard?"

"Yes." Brandon nodded. "If I buy it and it becomes my backyard."

"But you wouldn't want to live with Josh," Jodie said. "He's messy and you're tidy."

"I'm okay with mess as long as I'm allowed to tidy it up if I want to."

Hallie smiled and looked out the window. "He is messy, isn't he?"

"It's kind of ironic." Brandon's chuckle was sad.

"What?"

"For years, Mom would say, 'Tidy your room, Brandon. You don't want to end up like the Junk Man.' And I'd tidy my room. Now I'm not so sure that being like the Junk Man would be such a horror after all."

Looks passed between Josh and Hallie.

Finally Hallie cleared her throat. "I don't have a problem with it."

"Me either."

"You don't mind the noise of my dad's geese? You're not worried about rats and mice?"

Josh shook his head. "Never seen any rats or mice here. And the geese are fine. If you want to buy this place and use the backyard, go for it."

"I guess it would mean Bandit shouldn't be here," Hallie said. "Cats and squirrels don't mix. But he can stay at the Ladans. Lil spoils him." She looked at Jodie. "And so do you."

Jodie lifted her chin. "Well, he kept going around the house meowing for Josh when he moved out. I felt sorry for him, and he loves those little sardine treats with catnip. He needed a bit of spoiling."

"Josh or Bandit?" Brandon quipped.

Jodie patted his cheek and smiled into his eyes. "I'll let you work that one out."

He grinned then looked around the room. "So we're all good?"

"Happy," Jodie said, getting up from his lap. "But not good. Where are the choc-chip cookies?" She made a dash for the kitchen. Josh scrambled after her and grabbed her arm. He half-dragged, half-carried his struggling sister back to Brandon and dumped her on his lap.

"Hold her, would you?"

"With pleasure." Brandon locked his arms around Jodie's waist and drew her against his chest. She leaned back, not bothering to struggle, and rested her head under his chin.

"I'm not that hungry anyway."

He loosened his grip and moved his face close to hers. "I am," he whispered, his eyes darkening with meaning.

"Not in front of my brother," she whispered back.

He smiled into her eyes, then peered around her to see Josh and Hallie. "Well, it's been lovely and all, but I think it's time Jodie and I headed off."

"I can't even tempt you with some choc-chip cookies?" Hallie held up the packet.

"Nah." Brandon stood, gently removing Jodie from his lap but not letting go of her waist. "I've got something better." He winked at Jodie.

Blushing furiously, she grabbed his hand and tugged him out the door.

They'd only reached the bottom step when Brandon pulled her into his arms and kissed her. He loved the feel of her in his arms, her sweet acceptance and … her fierce passion. His eyes shot open as she pressed against him, as though she desired him as much as he desired her.

"Jodie." He gently pushed her back, putting space between them. "I … I um, think we better go ask my dad what he thinks about me buying this place."

Jodie looked up at him, her expression a mixture of wonder and adoration. She nodded.

"That sounds like a wise idea."

CHAPTER TWENTY-EIGHT

"Would it work?" Brandon asked his father, eyes full of hope.

Luke didn't answer at first. He focused on feeding Edward the squirrel, handing him nuts one at a time.

Jodie's heart sped up. Surely Brandon's dad would approve of Brandon buying the cottage and land next door? It seemed so perfect. Yet she was learning God's ways were not always her ways, His wisdom not the same as the world's.

"How did you say we'd fund it?" He handed Edward another nut. The squirrel took it from his fingers and nibbled daintily.

"Marla and Rhonda want to start a fundraiser. They've got all kinds of ideas."

Luke grunted. "I'd prefer they knitted blankets for the critters. That'd be more useful."

"Those two can be loose cannons," Brandon said with a grin.

"More like meteorites heading for the earth at a hundred thousand miles a second."

Jodie giggled at Luke's expression. Despite his gruff words, she detected fondness for the meddling women.

"What do you think?" Brandon asked.

Luke stopped feeding Edward and turned to look directly at his son. "I'm touched, actually. Touched you would do that for me. But I don't know that you should be using your money like that."

"Dad, you're the only family I've got. Are we going to have this whole argument again, like when you wouldn't accept a new truck from me?"

Luke made a noise that sounded like half chuckle, half snort. "You didn't give me a choice. Is that what you're saying? You'll override whatever I say anyway?"

"No." Brandon's shoulders fell and he rubbed the back of his neck. "I really want to know what you think. I want to do what's right."

"I know." His dad rubbed the back of his neck in a manner so like Brandon's that Jodie smiled.

A knock came at the door and Luke stood, grumbling as he did so. Jodie shot an amused look at Brandon and his mouth tipped in return.

"That's what you'll be like when you're older," Jodie said quietly, nodding in the direction his dad had gone.

"Pfft," Brandon tried to look disgusted, but his eyes were twinkling.

Their attention was drawn to the voices at the door.

"Luke McAffrey, long time no see," a booming voice said.

"Wayne. It's been way too long. Please come in."

There came the sound of the door opening and heavy boot-steps down the hall.

"This is my son Brandon, and his friend Jodie," Luke said as the tall man stepped in the door. "Brandon and Jodie, Wayne Gilbertson."

Wayne's eyes widened. "Well, well, I'd heard the rumors, but I can see for myself it's true. You are indeed Luke's son. And my cousin, too."

Brandon shuffled uncomfortably, looking down at his hands.

"Yeah, well, I'm not sure how it works, but my mom Mariah was your cousin."

Wayne beamed. "Exactly. I count you as family."

Jodie made a scoffing noise. She couldn't help it. "Since when?"

Wayne's eyes darted to her, then back to Luke and Brandon. "I know I could have managed things better in the past. I can make all kinds of excuses about why I did what I did, but I want to say I'm sorry for the difficulty it caused you. And Mariah. I tried to make it right for Mariah, and I want to make it right for you too."

Yeah. With money. Jodie wanted to scoff again. There would be money involved, she knew it. That's how people like Wayne and Susannah Gilbertson worked. They might not be married anymore, but some things never changed.

"Do you think paying for Mariah's nurse made things right?" she asked.

The blood drained from Wayne's face, and everyone stared at her. She swallowed. She should have thought before she spoke.

Wayne cleared his throat and looked at the floor. "She was my cousin," he said, his voice now quiet. "I loved her."

Brandon's mouth dropped open. "It was you? She accepted it from you?"

"Not without a fight." Wayne pinched the bridge of his nose. "But it was the least I could do."

"How—how did you convince her?" Brandon's expression was incredulous.

Wayne chuckled, a sad sound. "Reminded her she had you to look out for. It surprised me she accepted it, to be honest, but she'd changed. There was a … humility, a graciousness in her. She said she had prayed for help, so if God sent it through me she had no right to refuse it."

Well. Jodie looked at Brandon. He still looked stunned.

Wayne looked back to Luke. "But the reason I'm here is that I've heard my ex-wife is causing you grief. And I have a plan."

Luke remained standing, and Jodie realized there weren't enough seats in the room. She went to stand, but Wayne waved her back down.

"No, no, you stay there. This won't take long." He looked at Luke. "I want to offer you some land on the edge of the golf course to rehabilitate your birds. Marla and Rhonda Ingalls have come to me with a mighty fine-looking plan they want me to fund, but it's too big for the space in your yard, and I'm well aware of the new council regulations."

Jodie grinned. "I've seen the plans. It's a palace for geese."

"My geese don't want a palace, and I don't either." Luke looked at her, then Wayne.

She felt both guilty and ignorant, but Brandon reached for her hand and squeezed reassuringly.

"What do you want?" Wayne asked Luke. "Name it and its yours."

"I want to live with integrity. I want peace in my soul. I want to do what's right." Luke was shorter than Wayne, but he looked so much taller as he gazed seriously at Wayne.

Wayne slumped like a deflated balloon. "I'm trying to give you that."

"Only God can give me that, and He has. Wayne, what's done is done. I appreciate that you're trying to make it right, but I'm okay. In fact, I'm better than okay. I have a son any father would be proud of, I have a job I love, cleaning up the filth humans leave behind and making the world a better place. I'm happy."

Wayne blinked, then ran a hand through his thinning hair. "I believe you, Luke, but as a friend, if I can help you in any way …"

"Actually," Luke said, "My son could do with your advice and experience about a property he's considering buying."

Brandon looked stunned but pulled himself together. "Yeah.

I'd prefer you didn't tell Susannah, but I'm thinking of buying the cottage next door. It has enough room for Dad to keep ten geese, even with the new council regulations. I just … I have no idea about buying and selling property."

"I'd be delighted to help." Wayne was positively beaming. "And if you're dealing with Bob Ingalls, he knows I don't put up with nonsense. I'll get you a deal better than you thought possible."

Brandon blinked a couple of times, then let out a big sigh. "You have no idea how much I'd appreciate that."

Luke looked thoughtful. "And we don't want your money, but we could do with manpower. If you'd consider helping build …" He looked at Brandon and winked, "a squirrel ninja warrior course I'd be most grateful."

Wayne's eyebrows flew up. "A … a what did you say?"

"Squirrel playground. Obstacle course. Whatever. Brandon got me watching Mark Rober, and I'm impressed."

"Mark who?"

"A YouTuber."

Wayne looked completely lost, and Jodie felt a giggle building up. She coughed, trying to hold it back, but it wouldn't cooperate. What came out was a burst of noise halfway between a squirrel's bark and a donkey's bray.

All eyes turned to her and she shook her head, trying to contain herself.

Brandon took her hand and patted it. "Don't mind Jodie. She's got a strange sense of humor."

"I see," Wayne said, but it was clear he didn't. He looked between them all again, then held out his hand for Luke to shake. "Well, Luke, it's great to see you and hear that you're doing so well. I'll be in touch. I'd like to see more of my girls, so I'll be around a bit more."

"No worries." Brandon's father shook the man's hand and led him out the front door.

Jodie burst into giggles again, and Brandon chuckled. "You good?"

Luke smiled as he came back into the room, and his eyes were warm. "She's living life to the full. It wouldn't hurt you to giggle once in a while, son. You're too serious."

"What?"

Luke grinned. "I was inclined to giggle myself when Wayne looked around as though we'd lost our minds."

Brandon shook his head. "I think the truth is, I've finally found mine." A slow grin formed. "Thanks, God."

Luke nodded. "Thanks, God."

CHAPTER TWENTY-NINE

It had been a huge six weeks. Jodie walked around the cottage yard with Brandon and his father as they discussed plans. Wayne had been a huge blessing, the way he'd supported Brandon, negotiated a good deal on the cottage and advocated for him every step of the way, right through to the end of sale. Now they were waiting for the settlement date.

Jodie smiled. The days had been good. Enjoyable days of working with Selena, summer evenings and weekends with Brandon, packing up his mother's house which had also been sold. She and Brandon had gone to Spokane one Saturday and Brandon had driven her around the raceway. She'd been genuinely impressed with his driving skills as he sped around the circuit.

Then they'd visited Esther together. She seemed well and happy. She said Mark wasn't moving to New York after all, and she was waiting to see if her transfer could be cancelled.

Yet Jodie still struggled to believe everything was okay with her sister. Esther spoke of her faith and trust in God, but Jodie knew how much could be hidden behind a spiritual front. And she didn't miss how Esther drew the attention away from herself at every opportunity.

"I think the squirrel gym should go there." Brandon pointed, drawing her attention back to the present.

Luke suggested another option closer to a tree. Jodie had never seen him so animated. He and Brandon seemed more alike by the day.

"I don't know how to go about getting the money together," Luke said. "I know Wayne will give any money we ask for, but we don't want the town to think there's something fishy going down."

"Even if the waterbirds like the sound of that."

Jodie groaned. Brandon's jokes were worse than Dad's.

"Luke," she said. "Marla and Rhonda were onto something with their ideas for getting the community involved, but it needs a little more ..."

"Finesse?" Luke asked, a twinkle in his eyes.

"Yes. I need to ask Selena if I can write an article about our town's need for a wildlife refuge. I'll write about the potential of this place, citing how it's close to the lake but far enough from the busy tourist areas for animals to recuperate. I'll say how you're the best person for the job, but I'll ask for volunteers, both to help you care for the animals and to keep the place tidy. We could have rosters for mowing, work days, barn raising—"

"Barn raising?" Brandon chuckled.

"You know what I mean. Shed and aviary raising. If we get the town on board, Susannah will leave you alone. She's all about appearances. She cares what people think of her. We could even suggest that her concern about rats and mice is valid and what a good thing she cared enough to raise the issue. Make it seem like she was in on the idea."

Luke chuckled.

"The Bible says to bless those who persecute us." Jodie grinned at him.

"Doesn't the Bible also call it heaping burning coals on your enemy's head?"

Brandon looked at his dad. "Would you like to do that?"

Luke smiled. "I find a lot of Jesus's teachings to be unconventional, but I like Him. He turns the world upside down and goes against the flow. Let's go bless an enemy, shall we?"

Jodie grinned. "Let's do it."

***

"It's a great idea," Selena said when Jodie shared her idea about writing an article encouraging the community to get behind Luke's wildlife rehabilitation scheme. "Anything to capture the interest of the town and bring everyone in Trinity Lakes together is exactly what we're aiming for. You saw the way the town got behind Ellie and the museum. That's what we want."

Jodie beamed. "Exactly."

"You can guide the research, but I'll need to write the article."

Disappointment filled Jodie. "What? Why?"

Selena chuckled. "Do you think people haven't noticed the way you and the Junk Man's son look at each other? We don't want them to think the article is biased, do we?"

Jodie bit her lip. "The Junk Man's name is Luke, but yeah, you could be right."

Selena laughed. "I am right. Let's get started on this article. I'll begin by interviewing the Junk— Luke and his son. You can come if you think you can keep your focus on work." Her eyes sparkled with teasing.

Jodie grinned. "I'll give it a go."

"Right. Well let's go ferret out some information, shall we?"

"You mean squirrel out?"

Selena's eyes widened, then she chuckled. "You're fun to work with, Jodie. I'm glad you've joined my team."

Jodie grinned. "Me too."

How could she have thought she'd prefer to be studying in New York? This was so much better—going out into the town she loved, interviewing people she loved, seeking the truth, speaking in love, and mixing justice with mercy.

Her heart was full and overflowing with gratefulness.

Thank you, Lord.

CHAPTER THIRTY

The office for the Trinity Lakes Gazette had been busy all morning. Even Selena was surprised by the response to her article and the number of people who wanted to help or donate. Most people registered their interest or donations online, but some had come into the office.

"I can offer free vet services if they're ever needed," the local vet, Jessica Martin, told them.

"We can come up with more ideas," Rhonda and Marla Ingalls said, placing even more elaborate pictures and plans on Selena's desk.

Jodie and Selena looked at one another, holding back smiles.

"I heard Luke say he could do with blankets for his animals," Jodie said.

Rhonda's eyes lit up. "We could do that. Let's start a knitting group. We'll even let anyone who wants to crochet come too."

"Crochet?" Marla made a disgusted noise in her throat. "What are you thinking, Rhonda? A goose is going to get its foot stuck in the holes of a crocheted blanket."

Rhonda lifted her chin. "Not necessarily. I'm sure we have people in town who can crochet without big holes."

Marla made a noise suspiciously like a growl. "What do you think crocheting is? You planning to have a blanket knit with steel wool as well? Knit the aviaries?"

Selena cleared her throat and coughed into her hand. "Ladies, we appreciate your ideas. How about you write them down and submit them to our online page?"

Rhonda and Marla's expressions immediately became radiant and they beamed at Jodie and Selena.

"I'm so glad you took on my idea," Marla said. "I knew it was God-given inspiration the moment I came up with it."

"You came up with it?" Rhonda's eyes were wide with indignation.

"We appreciate you both," Jodie said, relieved when more people came through the door. "Now, ladies, if you can go home and write out any other ideas you have … Hello Becky."

The two Ingalls ladies were still arguing as they left the building.

"Fun." Becky grinned.

"They mean well."

Becky laughed. "I know. I have an idea too. I'm hoping it's more helpful than—" She glanced after the two women. "Well, anyway … I'd like to provide free cupcakes and donuts for anyone helping with building or cleaning up the Junk Man's yard."

"Thank you." Jodie's mouth watered at the mere thought of Becky's delicious baking.

Becky leaned in close. "I hear my dad paid Luke McAffrey a visit."

"He did."

"Well, I thought you'd like to know, he's written a letter to the council suggesting they allow exemptions for wildlife caretakers. I read it, and it was a great letter. He wants Luke to be allowed up to twenty fowl at a time and as many animals as he sees fit. Dad has even offered to inspect Luke's property on behalf of the council at no charge."

"Really?" Jodie's heart lifted. God was good. He'd surrounded Luke with friends and was showing him what their loving Heavenly Father would do for His children.

Jodie took another look at the online donation page. The amount was growing by the hour.

Jasper Cohen and Joel Manning came into the office next.

"We'd like to help," Jasper said. "We have some building skills, and we can offer discounted materials from our store. We'll also put a fundraising box out the front and allow people to donate through the store."

Jodie found tears forming in her eyes. Overwhelmed, she nodded and asked them to go online and fill out their details and the skills they could offer.

The rest of the morning was filled with people contacting the newspaper office, hearts, and hands full and ready to give.

THE WORK BEGAN the day after final settlement on the sale of the cottage. Brandon grinned at each new helper as they turned up dressed and ready to help. He'd never seen the street so busy. Cars lined each side, with three pickups coming in and out, carrying new materials and carting old materials away.

People laughed and talked and called out to each other as they worked. Wayne Gilbertson oversaw the operation. Even Susannah turned up.

"How can I help?" she asked Brandon stiffly.

He grinned, looking her up and down. She wore a white dress suit, high heels, and a classy scarf around her neck. His mischievous streak wanted to suggest she clean geese droppings from the back path. Instead, he pointed to where Becky stood behind her bakery cart across the street. She'd set it up there for anyone who needed a coffee or something to eat.

"Maybe your daughter could do with some help?" Better to keep Susannah away from Wayne. They didn't need drama today, and who knew what Susannah would say or do to her ex-husband given the chance.

Susannah nodded, her mouth drawn in a tight line. "I can do that for a few minutes."

A few minutes. Brandon wanted to laugh, but it was a miracle she was even here. "Thank you for your support," he said as she turned to leave.

She nodded once with a haughty look on her face, a queen acknowledging her subjects.

"Susannah!" Marla and Rhonda waddled over at top speed, reminding Brandon of Dad's geese.

Susannah froze.

"Oh, you're wonderful," Marla said. "Thank you for coming and supporting our idea for this place. Isn't it amazing to see it all coming together?"

"Supporting the idea?" Deep creases formed in Susannah's brow. "I was the one who brought the need to light. Goodness gracious, if this place had continued the way it was …" She shook her head. "I made sure the council knew what was needed, and look how much good it's done."

Brandon's mouth dropped open. He shut it as quickly as he could, but words bubbled up. He wanted to speak the truth. How he wanted to speak the truth. But there was no love in any of the words that would come out.

Susannah turned to Brandon. "Thank goodness you've turned out more like your father than your mother."

That was it. "Many people feel the same about your daughters."

He could see her processing his words and would have said more, but a warm, gentle hand slipped into his.

"Brandon, can I see you for a minute?"

He looked down into Jodie's sweet face, her understanding eyes. God was providing a way out of temptation. She tugged on his hand and he followed.

"Jodie, you're an angel sent to save me," he said when she pulled him into his cottage, the only place not crawling with people.

"I don't know about that." She grinned and pulled his head down. "Angels don't do this."

And she kissed him, cooling the fire of anger and igniting another fire in his veins. The sooner he married this girl, the better.

———

BRANDON COULD HEAR the local tiler, Joel Manning, and a plumber climbing through the ceiling, calling out to one another as they traced the water damage.

He went to find Dad and found him watching some workers pour concrete where his old homemade bird aviaries had been. "Dad, Jasper and Joel said you won't be able to live here until they've finished. The more they look, the more leaks they find. They need to replace a section of the ceiling in your bedroom."

"You mean I have to move out of the place I said I'd never leave?"

"Yeah. Sorry." His guilt eased when he saw the twinkle in his father's eyes, softening his gruff tone. "You don't mind too much?"

Those intelligent green eyes studied him. "How could I? You and your friends tried to tell me God still administers justice and that he cares for the poor and fatherless. I didn't believe it at the time, but ...." He looked around. "How can I not believe it?"

Brandon smiled. His mom had found the same loving Father in God before she died. He had much to be thankful for.

He gave his dad a hug. "I'm so, so blessed to have you."

His dad considered him. "You're not ashamed of me?"

"No. I'm proud. So proud. You're the strongest man I know."

His dad looked at Jasper single-handedly carrying a sheet of drywall into the house and laughed.

"In character, I mean," Brandon said, grinning. "You have integrity. You stand for what's right. You're not burdened and trapped by what people think of you."

"There comes a point where you can't survive on what people think of you," Dad said. "Especially if you know you can't live up to their expectations."

"Yeah, I tried," Brandon said. "For a long time. I was determined to make my own way in the world, to prove myself to the Gilbertson side of the family, and to myself."

Dad rubbed his face where his beard was beginning to regrow. "They'd never admit it, but I think you've done it. Or God's done it. I'm not stupid. I have a good idea where the huge donation put into a trust to keep this property going came from."

"You think it came from Susannah?" Brandon's eye widened.

"Wayne. He won another golf tournament. He knew I wouldn't accept it from his hand, so sneaky man that he is, he found another way." Dad grinned, proving he wasn't really upset. He would do anything for his birds, including swallow his pride.

Brandon looked around at the cornices Jasper Cohen and his team were pulling down, then back to Dad. "Are you going to come and stay in my house until all this mess gets sorted out?"

"You calling this a mess?" Dad mock scowled.

"No. No, I meant ..."

Dad's face broke into a grin and he gave Brandon a playful punch. "I know what you meant. Yes, I'll grab the things I'll need for the next few days and come next door. I'll never say no to spending more time with my son."

Brandon's heart leapt. And yet, he was missing time with Jodie. It was clear he was going to have to carve out some time to spend alone with her.

———

JODIE WATCHED THE WORKERS, wishing she could help in some way. Brandon said she'd done enough by printing her article and helping arrange the fundraising and volunteers, but her hand still limited the physical work she could do. Brandon had suggested she could help his dad fend off all the people wanting to talk to him, but to her surprise, there was no need for that. He seemed to be enjoying the conversations, even instigating them.

"Did you know there are even people here from Spokane and Walla Walla?" Jodie asked him when he came aside to feed another orphaned squirrel someone had brought him. "You're famous now."

"Hmm." Luke held the tiny squirrel in his hand and squeezed milk into its mouth through a medicine dropper. 'I don't know that I like fame. I've been out of the social eye for so long it takes a bit of getting used to."

Jodie smiled. He might say that, but deep down she had a feeling he was enjoying the day.

Brandon came to join them, squeezing her in a side hug. "Is Dad teaching you how to feed baby squirrels?"

She laughed. "He doesn't trust me that much."

Luke looked up. "Who says I don't? You didn't ask."

Jodie looked at the tiny creature with barely any fur on it, eyes still closed. Its little paws held the dropper as it sucked the milk.

"Would you like to?" Luke asked.

"Um … it's so fragile."

He laughed. "This one fell out of a tree and survived. I don't think you need to worry."

"Okay." Jodie allowed Brandon to set the squirrel gently on her lap. He placed her hand over the top of it, while Luke passed her the dropper. The squirrel struggled against her hand, trying to reach the milk. She smiled at the feel of the little paws against her hand, and sat mesmerized as the tiny creature suckled the dropper.

"He's so perfect," she whispered.

"She, actually." Luke rubbed his chin. "I haven't come up with a name for her yet. Maybe Claudia."

Brandon laughed. "Where do you come up with these names? Is that what you would have called a daughter had you had one?"

Luke grinned affectionately at Brandon. "No, she would have been Gertrude."

"Seriously?" Brandon's brows shot up and Jodie giggled, seeing the twinkle in his dad's eyes.

Luke shook his head. "Now see here, son, this is the way rumors start. Assumptions, misunderstandings—"

"Bad jokes," Brandon cut in.

"That too."

Jodie looked between them, then down at little Claudia in her lap. What a family. She'd love to become part of this family someday. She couldn't love them more than she already did. A little boy who looked just like Brandon wouldn't be a bad thing, either. Her heart warmed at the thought.

Brandon nudged her shoulder. "What's that look for?"

She shrugged, focusing on the little squirrel beneath her hand. No way was she going to scare him away with thoughts of marriage and children.

Brandon squatted down beside her until he was eye level and his gaze captured hers.

"Being a mother suits you."

She caught her breath at the tenderness in his gaze. How could she have considered leaving this town? Leaving him? How could she have ever thought him insensitive and immature?

"I love you, Brandon," she murmured.

His slow smile had her heart beating faster, every part of her captivated by the man that he was.

"I love you, too," he whispered before touching his lips to her brow. "And I hope that one day we have lots of our own little squirrels running around."

She laughed and Claudia startled beneath her hand. Luke reached over and took her.

"Let Grandpa Luke take her for a bit. You two obviously need a few moments alone."

CHAPTER THIRTY-ONE

Jodie looked up from the computer as the front door of the Trinity Lakes Gazette office opened. Brandon. She smiled as he walked in, the smell of gasoline wafting from his work clothes.

"You'd better not come in here." Selena looked over from her desk. "Between that gas or whatever it is on your clothes and the sparks flying between you two, it's not safe."

"Ha ha." Brandon grinned, but his eyes were locked on Jodie's.

"May I help you, sir?" she asked, putting on her most posh accent.

"Yes, I believe you may." He came around the front desk and planted a kiss on her lips. "Thank you. I needed that."

Selena stood, shoving the papers in front of her to the side. "Come on, you two. Get married already."

"Now that's not a bad idea." Brandon's eyes lit. He looked down at Jodie. "What do you reckon, Jodes? We could kick your brother out of my cottage, move in, and live happily ever after."

They could. It sounded like the perfect idea, but she kept that to herself. Brandon had been hinting about marriage more often lately, but she could never tell when he was serious and when he wasn't. She wasn't going to take anything for granted.

Brandon stood and leaned against Jodie's desk. "I am actually here for a purpose."

Selena's brows rose. "Really?"

"Yeah." He wiped his hands down his jeans. "I have something to prove."

"Oka-ay." Selena grinned and Jodie wondered what was coming. She never knew with Brandon, but she loved that about him. He was exciting. Unpredictable. Full of new ideas for adventure.

He handed Selena his phone. "I need you to record this."

"What?"

"Record me. Jodie and me."

"Riight ..." Shaking her head, Selena lifted the phone.

Brandon squatted down beside Jodie again, his face level with hers once more. His eyes were twinkling with merriment as they captured hers. He lifted a hand and ran it down her face. Gently, tenderly.

She couldn't help smiling into his eyes. "What's this proving?"

"That you love me no matter what. Bruce and Ryder reckoned you wouldn't come near me if I came home every day smelling like this the rest of my life, but I told them you're different. They didn't believe me."

Jodie sputtered out a laugh. "They sent you here?"

"No, I came of my own accord. I had something to prove to them."

Jodie put her arms around his neck and ran her fingers through his thick, messy dark hair. She breathed in the smell of him and smiled.

"You can tell them I'm different. I love everything about you. Even the grease and fuel."

Then she tugged him closer and kissed him thoroughly.

Finally she pulled back, vaguely aware of Selena's voice in the background.

"Can I stop recording now, or do I have to watch more of this … this display?"

"Depends." Brandon grinned at her. "Do you think I have enough proof?"

Selena snorted. "You could turn up smelling like a skunk, and she wouldn't notice."

Brandon stood and Jodie missed the warmth of his touch. He reached for his phone.

"Thank you, Selena. Job done."

"Job done?" Jodie pretended to be offended. "Kissing me is work to you? Is that what —"

Before she could finish, he grabbed her up from the chair, plonked himself down and pulled her into his lap. She laughed and pushed against his chest, but her laugh was cut off by his lips on hers again. This time soft and slow and deliberate. She found herself caught up with him, drowning in the feel of him, the smell of him, the taste of him. She was completely consumed by all that was Brandon.

When he pulled back, she let out a shaky breath and stared at him, dazed. He put his work-roughened hands either side of her face and smiled into her eyes.

"Didn't feel like work to me. How about you?"

No. Definitely not work. She'd tell him when she'd recovered her senses enough to speak.

Selena cleared her throat. "I hate to interrupt such an intimate moment, but I'm paying Jodie by the hour."

"Yeah yeah. I'm going." Brandon gently lifted Jodie from his lap and stood. His eyes met hers. "I love you."

"I love you, too."

Then he walked back out the door.

EPILOGUE

Brandon looked out his window at the graying skies and shivered. Not because fall was already halfway through and winter was on its way, but because he'd never been more nervous in his life. His dad straightened his tie for him. "You'll be fine. That girl loves you so much she can't see straight."

"What's that supposed to mean? If she could see me properly, she wouldn't love me?"

Dad laughed and patted his shoulder. "No. You're a very handsome man—"

"Who looks just like you," Brandon finished with a grin. "Yeah, I know."

"At least you don't smell like cars tonight."

"Yeah, I'm clean. I used that Honest-to-Goodness cleanser Jodie gave me." Brandon held up his hands. He'd been surprised how well the product worked.

His father placed both hands on his shoulders and Brandon found himself looking into eyes much like his own. "I'm proud of you son," Dad said. "So proud. Go with God tonight, confident in who you are. His child. Dearly loved."

"Thank you." Brandon swallowed hard. He'd been deeply

moved when Dad had sat and prayed with him earlier, asking God to direct his words and bless his love for Jodie. Theo Ladan had done the same when he'd asked permission to marry her. Josh had given his blessing too, and even suggested a double wedding. He was surrounded by family who supported him, valued him, and loved him. He was blessed beyond measure.

Memories flashed as he drove to the Ladan home. The first time he'd seen Jodie bouncing down the stairs at the Ladan home, ponytail swinging. The first time he'd heard her laugh. The first time she'd set her blazing blue eyes on him and told him off.

He took his hands off the wheel one at a time to wipe them down his jeans. She could be fierce when she believed in something. But that also meant she loved fiercely.

He pulled in the Ladans' driveway the way he had many times before. But this time was not like the others. His future depended on this night.

The door opened the moment he knocked. Jodie stood there, wearing a stunning sapphire blue dress with a split up the side that showed off her figure to perfection. Her golden-blonde hair was flowing down her shoulders, a few tendrils whispering against her face. He met her blue eyes and his breath caught. She was beautiful. In every way. The more he got to know her, the more he loved her compassion, her strong sense of justice, and her giving heart that first and foremost beat with love for God. And then him.

She threw her arms around him as though she'd been as desperate to see him as he was to see her.

"You're here." She kissed him, then kissed him again.

"I'm here." Funny how all his nerves disappeared the moment he was in her presence. "You ready?"

"Way ready."

He chuckled at her enthusiasm and walked out to the car

with her. She went to open the passenger door, but he got there first.

"Nuh uh, my job tonight."

She smiled. "Aren't you the perfect gentleman?"

"You know it."

He pulled her seat belt out for her, then closed the door and went around to his side of the truck. She chatted about the new restaurant in town as they drove. He tried to listen instead of rehearsing everything he wanted to say to her. His hand went up to touch the box in his pocket. Still there.

"Ooh," Jodie said when she saw the way the restaurant lit up in the evening sky. "It's beautiful."

Maybe it was, but he was having trouble keeping his eyes off her. The joy and wonderment he saw in her expression made him feel so alive.

She waited for him to open the door for her this time and held his hand as they walked up the steps to Giovanni's Italian Restaurant. It had only been open a month, and he'd had to book two weeks ahead. Two weeks of nervous waiting.

"Table for McAffrey-Taylor," Brandon said. Jodie stared at him, just as he knew she would, but she didn't say anything.

She settled into the seat across from him and picked up the menu. He gently tugged it from her fingers and met her blue-eyed gaze. He answered the question there.

"I was just trying out the name. I wanted to see how you like it."

"McAffrey?"

"Yes."

"It's an honorable name."

"I went to the district court and got some forms. A petition to change my name."

Her eyes sparkled. "Oh Brandon, that's so special. Your dad must be pleased."

"I haven't done it yet."

"Oh?"

"No, I have something to ask you first." He stood up from the table, drew the small box from his pocket and kneeled in front of her. "Jodie-Lee Ladan, will you marry me?"

She smiled wide and her eyes filled with tears. "You know I will."

He grinned. "A simple yes will do."

"Yes."

He slid the ring onto her finger, then stood and drew her into his arms, kissing away the tears dripping from her eyes.

"Next question," he said, "Would you prefer to be a Taylor or a McAffrey?"

She laughed. "Either? Both? I will take whatever name you have. Your name will be my name, your home will be my home, your God will be my God."

He chuckled. Quoting Ruth from the Bible. Such a pastor's daughter.

"McAffrey sounds kind of distinguished, don't you think?" She patted his chest affectionately.

It did. He covered her hand, holding it against his chest. He had more to say. "I, Brandon James McAffrey, promise you, Jodie-Lee Ladan, that in all my days on earth I will never leave you. If one of us goes home to heaven before the other, it will only be 'see you later,' never goodbye forever. I will share this life with you every day I live here on earth, and I will share eternity with you in heaven."

She let out a small sob and buried her face in his jacket. He held her tighter, protectiveness and love burning like fire in his veins. He'd never known he could love like this. Never known he could be the type of man who was worthy of such a woman.

She pulled back and sniffed, wiping her nose with the back of her hand. He grinned. That was his Jodie. He reached over, grabbed a napkin and placed it in her hand.

"You want to know the truth?" she asked as she wiped her nose on the napkin.

He nodded.

"I think I've loved you from the moment I set eyes on you. Back when I was a little fifteen-year-old girl."

"Ah, Jodie," he said with a smile. "You weren't a little girl. For as long as I've known you, you've been a strong, independent woman who knows her mind and spits fire if anyone gets in her way."

She shook her head, reaching a hand to rest it on the side of his face. "Not anymore. I don't want to be independent if it means being apart from you. And you could never get in my way. Never again."

He smiled. "We'll see." There were sure to be times he frustrated her and vice versa. But with everything within him he was going to fight to put her first. To meet her needs and always speak the truth in love. Because the truth was, this love he felt for her went way deeper than feelings. It had become a part of him, a part of God within him, and he knew he would die to save her if he needed to.

But he didn't need to. God had done that for both of them already. Now all that was left was life. Life beyond all he had ever dreamed.

"Turn to face the camera, you two," a familiar voice said.

Brandon and Jodie turned at the same time to see Selena holding her camera.

"Beautiful," she said. "Now turn and face each other. Hold hands, but tilt them so I can see the ring."

They did as she asked. Jodie let out a little sigh of contentment, and he couldn't help leaning down to steal a kiss.

"Hey," Selena said, but they ignored her. Brandon wrapped his arms around Jodie and her arms slid around him, pulling him closer.

"You smell good." She nuzzled his ear.

He chuckled and pulled back. "There are people watching," he whispered.

"I don't care." She shot him a cheeky grin before turning to face the people in the restaurant. "Just in case nobody knows, I love this man. He's a good man. A godly man. I trust him. Completely. And I can't quite believe I get to marry him." She winked at him. "And that's the truth."

Brandon chuckled. "I think you've just stolen Selena's thunder," he said softly, drawing her back into his arms as the people in the restaurant clapped and cheered.

"I don't know about thunder," she said, her blue eyes gazing into his. "But I sure feel like there are sparks bringing this place alive."

Alive indeed. He'd never felt so alive. The truth was, he never dreamed he'd know such love. And that was the honest-to-goodness truth.

THE END

If you enjoyed this book, stay tuned for Esther's story in *Like Stars That Shine*

Next in the series: Blue Skies Dreaming by Amanda Deed

A NOTE FROM THE AUTHOR

Thank you for reading *In Truth and Love,* my second book in the Trinity Lakes series. Jodie and Brandon's story was a joy to write, but some scenes were heart-wrenching too. I love how God writes the story of our lives and I know that in times of sorrow He grieves with us, but as the master author, He also knows that ultimately, all will be made beautiful in His time. He is the author or redemption.

If you enjoyed this book, get ready for Esther's story in *Like Stars That Shine,* coming April 2025.

I love hearing from my readers, so please feel free to email me: jenny@jennyglazebrook.com

Please also be sure to check out the other books in the Trinity Lakes series:

1. *Never Find Another You* by Narelle Atkins
2. *The Ocean Between Us* by Meredith Resce
3. *I'll Always Choose You* by Lisa Renee
4. *Always By My Side* by Iola Goulton
5. *Love Somebody Like You* by Carolyn Miller
6. **Where Our Hearts Lie by Jenny Glazebrook**
7. *No Matter How Far* by Sara Beth Williams

8. *Over the Rainbow* by Meredith Resce
9. *Tangled up in Love* by Carolyn Miller
10. *In Truth and Love* by Jenny Glazebrook
11. *Blue Skies Dreaming* by Amanda Deed
12. *Yesterday, Now and Always* - Sara Beth Williams
13. *Right in Front of You* - Jessica Wakefield
14. *Always in My Heart* by Iola Goulton
15. *Only You Can Love Me* - Carolyn Miller

You can purchase them here.

If you enjoyed *In Truth and Love*, please check out my website https://www.jennyglazebrook.com/ to find out more about me and my writing.

———

Reviews help other readers find new-to-them authors, so I'd really appreciate it if you can spare a moment to write a quick review at Goodreads or your place of purchase.

Next in the Trinity Lakes Romance series

Book #11 - *Blue Skies Dreaming* by Amanda Deed

The first time Nick Gordon met Violet Reynolds, he knew she was the one.

But now, one year later, after travelling from Australia to Trinity Lakes, Washington State, she doesn't want to have anything to do with him. And worse than that, she is already seeing someone else. Should he give up and go home, or see out the American summer as a skydiving instructor?

Violet is confused about who she is and what she wants in life, despite a wealthy legacy behind her. The trouble is, she doesn't feel suited to her tycoon daddy's wishes for her. And the fact that the cute guy, who duped her in Australia a year ago, has landed in her town, is not helping.

When Violet turns up as one of Nick's skydiving clients, he sees it as a godsend. But can he win her heart despite her doubts about him, despite the fact she is seeing someone, and most of all, despite her father's opposition? Can he learn to leave the outcome in God's hands?

A love-at-first-sight, small town contemporary Christian romance. Book 11 of the Trinity Lakes Romance series (can be read as a standalone). Visit Trinity Lakes and meet the fun and quirky characters who value family, faith, and happily-ever-afters.

Welcome to Trinity Lakes, the warm and welcoming small town in east Washington state filled with charm, family, and friends, where fresh starts, second chances, and romance abounds. You'll meet cowboys and swoony bachelors, sweet and sassy ladies, and your new best friends. This series of sweet and clean standalone Christian romances will warm your heart, inspire your faith, and bring a smile to your soul.

Check out the other books in the Trinity Lakes series:

Never Find Another You - Narelle Atkins

The Ocean Between Us - Meredith Resce

I'll Always Choose You - Lisa Renee

Always By My Side - Iola Goulton

Where Our Hearts Lie - Jenny Glazebrook

No Matter How Far - Sara Beth Williams

Over the Rainbow - Meredith Resce

Tangled Up in Love - Carolyn Miller

In Truth and Love - Jenny Glazebrook

Blue Skies Dreaming - Amanda Deed

Yesterday, Now and Always - Sara Beth Williams

Right in Front of You - Jessica Wakefield

Always in My Heart - Iola Goulton

Only You Can Love Me - Carolyn Miller

Like Stars That Shine - Jenny Glazebrook

ACKNOWLEDGMENTS

I am so blessed to have an amazing team around me who critique, proofread, edit and beta read my stories. I thank God for every one of you.

In particular I'd like to thank:

My fellow Trinity Lakes authors:

Meredith Resce and Sara Beth Williams - for your insightful comments and critique on this story.

Iola Goulton - for professionally critiquing and editing this story to an incredibly high standard.

Carolyn Miller - for your priceless mentoring, editing, formatting and encouragement. I have learned so much from you. Thank you for sharing your extensive experience, skills and gifting. I appreciate you more than I can say.

My friends from Christian Mommy Writers:

Hannah Hood Lucero - for proofreading both my Trinity Lakes novels. I love how you get the heart of my stories.

A special thank you to Heather Pine whose in-depth critique of both my Trinity Lakes stories has been invaluable. Thank you also for picking up when my Australianisms crept in. If anyone needs an in-depth critique of their manuscript, or someone to help them with US culture and expression, I encourage you to contact Heather.

My family:

My husband Rob – for reading the many drafts of my manuscripts and encouraging and supporting me along the way.

My daughter Clarity - who amazes me with the way she is both creative and logical and picks up so many things the rest of us have missed.

My son Micah and daughter Merridy – for your insightful comments and proofreading.

My daughter Amy – for the life and joy and delight you bring.

My mother Denise Crooks – for your proofreading and encouragement.

My friends:

Jenny Blake – for inspiring the idea of the squirrel.

Melanie Koch – for your proofreading and encouragement.

Most importantly, I thank my Lord and Savior, Jesus, for giving me hope, purpose and life. I am so blessed to be able to use the writing gift He has given me as both worship of Him and encouragement for others. He makes my life rich and beautiful and His presence brings such joy and hope, deepening my faith through every trial.

ABOUT THE AUTHOR

Jenny Glazebrook lives in a small country town in Australia. She and her husband Rob have four children and many rescue animals who fill their lives with joy.

Jenny writes stories which capture what it means to know Jesus and live for Him in a broken world.

She has a Diploma of Theology, is a qualified chaplain and experienced inspirational speaker. She loves to encourage others to understand God's love, see His hand in their lives, and walk with Him each day.

More about Jenny Glazebrook can be found on her website: https://www.jennyglazebrook.com/

ALSO BY JENNY GLAZEBROOK

The Trinity Lakes Series (Christian romance)

Where Our Hearts Lie

In Truth and Love

Like Stars that Shine (coming April 2025)

The Aussie Sky Series (YA fiction):

Blaze in the Storm

Heart of Thunder

Clouds of Prayer

Mist of the Morning

Clinging to Rainbows

Forgiving Sky

The Bateman Family Novels (YA/new adult fiction):

Daring Clare

Saving Beth

Framing Fleur

Seeing Jess

Living Melody

Loving Zoe (coming soon)

Other books

How The World Turns (coming 2024)

Molly the Dog-Sheep and other true pet parables (coming soon)

Collaborative works:

Wellspring Devotional Journal

Dear Jesus Diaries

More about Jenny her books can be found at <u>www.</u> <u>jennyglazebrook.com</u>